Stay Here with Me

Special Edition

The Wilder Bothers
Book 5

Carrie Ann Ryan

STAY HERE WITH ME

A WILDER BROTHERS NOVEL

By

Carrie Ann Ryan

STAY HERE WITH ME
A Wilder Brothers Novel
By: Carrie Ann Ryan
© 2022 Carrie Ann Ryan

Paperback ISBN 978-1-63695-193-5
Cover Art by Sweet N Spicy Designs
Photo by Wander Aguiar Photography

Praise for Carrie Ann Ryan

"Count on Carrie Ann Ryan for emotional, sexy, character driven stories that capture your heart!" – Carly Phillips, NY Times bestselling author

"Carrie Ann Ryan's romances are my newest addiction! The emotion in her books captures me from the very beginning. The hope and healing hold me close until the end. These love stories will simply sweep you away." ~ NYT Bestselling Author Deveny Perry

"Carrie Ann Ryan writes the perfect balance of sweet and heat ensuring every story feeds the soul." - Audrey Carlan, #1 New York Times Bestselling Author

"Carrie Ann Ryan never fails to draw readers in with passion, raw sensuality, and characters that pop off the page. Any book by Carrie Ann is an absolute treat." – New York Times Bestselling Author J. Kenner

"Carrie Ann Ryan knows how to pull your heartstrings and make your pulse pound! Her wonderful Redwood Pack series will draw you in and keep you reading long into the night. I can't wait to see what comes next with the new generation, the Talons. Keep them coming, Carrie Ann!" –Lara Adrian, New York Times bestselling author of CRAVE THE NIGHT

STAY HERE WITH ME

The Wilder Brothers from NYT Bestselling Author Carrie Ann Ryan continues with a secret romance that East and Lark never saw coming.

The world thinks I only write songs about my ex-boyfriends.

They study each lyric to point a finger at which man broke my heart—even if I've never met him.

Only the man I refuse to write about is the one who is so tangled in my mind that I know I can never be with him.

I had one night with East Wilder, and I know that's all there will ever be.

He broke my heart without even trying.

Yet now I can't seem to write a single verse and I need

a place to hide while I figure out who I am. The Wilder Retreat will have to be my refuge as the Wilders prepare for my best friend's wedding.

And when I'm there, I refuse to fall for East again.

Even if the dark shadows in his eyes draw me in and the dangers of his past might be the one thing that forces us to finally give in.

To Mariah.

Thank you for being my sounding board. And here is to our futures.

Chapter One

Lark

"I gave myself to the future you brought but you took what you wanted and never looked back. For I am nothing, nothing in your eyes. But I am everything in mine."
  "Without You" written by Lark Thornbird

I sat on the floor cross-legged, feet bare, and cursed the mountains of notebooks surrounding me.

This didn't make any sense. This was not me. I knew what I was doing. I had done this before, after all.

Yet it was like I had never written a lyric in my life.

I was a songwriter. It was part of who I was: a singer-songwriter.

I had Grammys for my writing, Billboard Music

Awards, and countless other smaller awards. I'd even won a Teen Choice Award for my song from a movie with America's favorite teen heartthrob.

That teen heartthrob was actually a twenty-five-year-old man who had kissed me on my cheek when I won, and with that kiss, he'd become my next Internet Boyfriend.

I rubbed my temples, cursing.

He was two years older than me, and yet they had called me a cougar because they assumed that with that boy-band hair, he was young and innocent.

If I had actually dated every single man that the internet accused me of, I wouldn't have had time to do anything else.

There was Brendan, the waiter from my favorite coffee shop. They assumed that I wrote "Without You" after he used me to get into that film.

Then James, the valet who used me to become a rockstar in his own right.

There were Bobby and Robert. Two completely different actors who were in a feud with each other, so of course, they put me in the middle.

There were Sebastian, Roger, Rourke, Timothy, Easton, Megan, Ariel, Eric, Aurora, Jasmine, John, Smith, Rory, Harry, and a few boy banders, just in the past three years alone.

Since I was fifteen—a full decade ago—when I wrote

my first song, I had been paired with nearly every current "It" boy and girl.

It didn't matter that I'd never been on a real date then, and the only boy I had ever kissed was from my hometown and who sold the story later to gain a few minutes of fame which had ruined my summer vacation.

Not that I actually got a summer vacation. I didn't get those.

But even through the fake heartbreaks and a few real ones, I had always been able to write.

And despite what others thought, I didn't usually have a real boy in mind—they were fictional. They were friendly until they were lyrics on a page that I could sing about.

I didn't need a man in order for me to make music.

After all, the internet would just make one up for me when it wanted to.

I was always able to write lyrics. I was good at it. Put a guitar in my hand and a mic in front of me, and I could sing. I could write. I could pour out my soul.

But I had nothing.

And I knew why.

I hated that I knew why.

"Damn that man."

Because there was a song in me I wanted to write. One that I thought I possibly needed to. But I wasn't

3

going to. I wouldn't write about him. *I couldn't.* I promised.

He thought I would anyway. He didn't trust me.

I trusted him with my body, let him inside me, and he didn't trust me not to break his heart. He believed what everyone else thought: That I used my heart and their soul to write my words, all so I could have fame and fortune and sell out stadiums. So I could have people tattoo my lyrics on their bodies so they could share a part of me. *They* wanted all of that, so of course I would use men and women to make that happen.

Of course, I would.

And East Wilder would believe all that. He wouldn't believe me.

I cringed and opened up my next notebook, reminding myself that I could do this. I was not going to freak out. I had *already* freaked out, but I wasn't going to think about that.

I rubbed my temples as my phone buzzed.

I looked down at the readout and ignored it. I did not want to talk to my manager. Yes, I had an album due soon. Yes, I needed to sit in the recording studio and record. But in order to do that, I needed songs.

And that just wasn't happening right now.

So instead, I picked up my phone and I tried to find another way out.

I wasn't going to run to him. I wasn't going to use him for inspiration. He was not my inspiration.

But maybe I needed a little something else.

Me: *Hey. Which home are you at right now?*

Bethany: *I'm in Texas. We just finished a shoot in LA, so I'm here for a couple of weeks before the wedding. Where are you?*

Me: *Vermont. I rented a room at a B&B. I am full of maple syrup, candy, and the scent of trees that I think are sending me into a full allergy attack.*

Bethany: *The allergies in San Antonio aren't great either. Are you doing okay?*

I hated that she understood me with just one text. But I shouldn't have been surprised.

Bethany Cole was my best friend. Had been my best friend for as long as I could remember. We'd started out in the business around the same time, and now she was an Academy Award-winning actress who did superhero movies, period pieces, and emotional drama pieces. She had even done a few comedies, which surprised everybody other than those who knew her.

Bethany was one of the best people I knew, and not just because of her talent.

And I needed my best friend just then.

I didn't know why. I should be fine. I had money, I had a home I loved, I had the ability to go wherever I needed to work. I was sitting here, alone on the floor, surrounded by my notebooks, and empty.

Just empty.

Me: *Do you think I can come down? Think I need a new view.*

Bethany: *Yes please! You're always welcome here. At our house, or one of the cabins. You know the Wilders would take care of you.*

I winced at that, because there was a certain Wilder I wanted to take care of me, and yet I knew he wouldn't. Which meant I didn't need him to. I didn't want to need him to.

There was something seriously wrong with me.

Bethany: *When are you getting into the studio?*

Bethany asked because we understood each other's careers, even though they were different.

Me: *Soonish. I have some time.*

Meaning I actually had to write songs first, but I wasn't going to think about that.

Bethany: *Come on down. The whole crew is here. We miss you. You're one of us.*

I snorted. I wasn't one of them. I was a friend, while everyone else was getting married or having babies. Bethany and Everett's wedding would be on the property soon, and I was the maid of honor so of course I was going to be there anyway. I would just get there early and hope for the best. I had to figure out something. Because sitting here and hoping to hell I could make this album work wasn't going to help me. Maybe I needed cowriters to write poems for me that I could somehow make my own. I had never needed that before. Even my coauthored songs had mostly come from me, and while I had done some duets, I had also done most of the writing. I was *good* at it. Sometimes it felt like it was the only thing I was good at. And yet, it wasn't working for me. And that scared me more than anything. Even more than the latest tabloid about me forever being alone because they hadn't seen me out and about with another human being in a while.

What if this was me being alone? What if I had nothing else to give?

The phone rang, and I immediately picked up, seeing Bethany's face.

"Okay, talk to me. What's wrong?"

I sigh. "I'm fine. Just having an off day."

Or an off week. Perhaps an off year.

Perhaps an off life.

"Well, I want to see you. It's been forever."

"It's been a month."

"That is forever. Come visit us. We love you."

I smiled. "Okay, I'll look up flights and figure out when I can get there. I don't think Vermont is working for me."

"Which is sad because Vermont is amazing, but if it's not working for you, it's not."

"When is your next movie?"

"We have to do reshoots for something soon. We were expecting it with the script changes."

I could practically hear her roll her eyes at that, but I just smiled into the phone. "And after that, anything new?"

"Enough. I think. It's going to be a long few months when things settle down. But I get a break because of the wedding and our honeymoon. I'm taking this thing called a vacation. I don't know if you've ever heard of it."

"I'm on vacation right now. What are you thinking? I'm covered in tree sap. It's beautiful."

Bethany's laughter soothed my soul. That was her. Just happiness personified. I knew that was in part because of her fiancé, but not all of it. A lot of it was the fact that Bethany was just an amazing light-filled soul who had gone through hell, and found her way out of it.

I loved her, and I was so happy for her.

I just wished I could find my own happiness. But that was on me.

And like most of my songs said, I did not need a man to make that happen.

"Okay. I'll see you soon. Give me all of your information, and we will make sure we pick you up."

"No, I can get there."

"No, you know one of the team is going to come to get you. We have to be careful with security."

I sighed but knew she was right.

Trace was her security specialist and bodyguard, and he had trained everyone that worked for her—and me when I needed it. He was also working to keep the Wilder Retreat safer. They had a few issues spring up over the years, not through any fault of their own, and with Bethany living on the compound and bringing some celebrity clientele with her, they had to be careful. So that meant I had to be careful, too.

"Okay, whatever you say. I'll see you soon."

"I'll see you soon. And then we can talk."

I was a little worried about that. I had my own secrets, and I knew Bethany was curious. She didn't pry. She wouldn't unless she thought I was hurting myself by not sharing.

I couldn't let her pry too much. Not when I was so afraid of what could happen. I hadn't told her about East.

The fact that I had slept with her future brother-in-law.

To be fair, she had six future brothers-in-law and at least three sisters-in-law at last count. Maybe four by this point. It was hard to keep up.

And I had slept with *him*. And it was a secret. The

biggest secret I had ever kept from my best friend. And I was not doing okay with it. And that should worry me.

Just a little bit.

By the time I touched down in San Antonio's small airport and made my way to the retreat on the other side of the city, I was tired, the cedar allergies hitting hard, and yet I finally felt like I was home.

I'd never once lived here, yet the sense the place gave me once I stepped on its clay soil spoke to me. Or perhaps they were merely lyrics waiting to get out of me.

Or the fact that my best friend lived here for part of the year.

We were in the Hill Country, and even though much of the grasses and plants were dormant right now, it was beautiful. The vineyard on the Wilder land was gorgeous, rolling over the hills, and the vines from other wineries surrounding them made a perfect picture.

I loved it here, the way that you could see for miles in some directions, and yet the hills blocked others.

Nothing beat a Texas sunset when you were feeling the need to look out into the future.

I quickly wrote down that line, even though I would have to alter it so it was a little more melodic. I was scraping the bottom of the barrel here, so I would use what I got.

We made our way through the gates and checked in with security at the front before pulling up to the main building of the Wilder Retreat and Winery.

I loved the Wilders. Not just the people but the place. There was a large inn where they had rooms, as well as a scattering of cabins on the property. There was a restaurant, gift shop, and multiple places for meetings and just for relaxation. You could take a golf cart, or walk through the greenery to get to the winery itself. My friend Maddie ran the tours there, and I knew some of the Wilders worked at the winery, and others at the inn or with event planning. One of my good friends now was the wedding planner for the whole place, because the Wilders hosted a lot of weddings. It was their main source of income for events.

I never would have thought that six big, brash, scarred, bearded, sexy, former military men would end up hosting weddings, but they were good at it.

I loved this place, with the limestone and white buildings, the black roofs that made it look modern and yet Texas ranch at the same time.

There was a new building being built over on the hill, one that I didn't recognize, but it had been a few months since I had been here. I'd have to ask Bethany what it was.

I got out of the electric town car and thanked the driver, as Bethany ran out from the front, blond hair waving, big sunglasses covering her face.

"You're here!"

I threw my arms around her and hugged her tight, ignoring the person with a cell phone taking a photo of us.

They were a guest and allowed to take photos. We didn't care at this point because if we had an issue with it, we wouldn't be standing in front of the building. If we had wanted to hide completely, we'd find a way.

I'm sure one of the staff members would politely mention something about privacy, but that didn't bother me.

I found privacy when I needed to.

I was grateful because I knew Bethany didn't have as much of a choice as I did.

People knew my voice and my face, but they didn't watch me day in and day out like they did her.

I didn't have a stalker like Bethany had.

"Come on. I'll show you to your cabin."

"Jason, do you mind getting her bags?"

"Of course."

"I'm good. I can handle it myself."

"No no, you're a guest. We're going to do everything like we would if you were a normal guest."

"Because I'm abnormal?" I rolled my eyes and she grinned.

"You said it. I didn't have to."

She kissed my temple, and we made our way down the path towards my favorite cabin. The little green one that nearly all of us had stayed in at one time or another.

It was like a show home, and yet filled with warmth.

I didn't always stay here, as it was highly sought after, but the fact that it would be my home for the next couple of days—or weeks—made me happy.

"You didn't have to give me this cabin."

"This is our favorite cabin for family and friends visiting. Plus, we have it open for now with the wedding coming up and the weeks ahead of time making sure we're all set to go."

"I love the fact that you're a *we*."

Bethany beamed, the light shining off her smile and that gorgeous diamond ring on her finger.

"I know, right? It's so weird to think about *we* as family, and not my team."

"Well, your team is here too, right?"

Bethany nodded. "At least Trace is for now. He's about to go back to LA to finalize a couple of things with the new bodyguards."

I frowned. "New?"

Bethany waved me off. "He's just in charge of training

the new members of the team so they can rotate in and out. I want them on Everett when we're out on things, too, and I think Trace is going to be working more with the people here. It's nice, because it doesn't feel like they're always around, you know?"

I nodded, knowing that sense of security was needed. And not just after everything she had gone through. We lived day in and day out with people wanting to know our every move.

"I wonder which security guard they're going to think I'm sleeping with now?" I asked as I rolled my eyes. I set my bag down, Jason following with the rest of the bags. I knew him from the security team, and he smiled, shaking his head.

"Not me, ma'am, if that's okay."

I blushed, shaking my head. "I think that was last year."

"And I'm very glad that I have an understanding wife. However, she also said if you need a beard, we've got you."

I groaned. "I cannot believe the paparazzi thought that we were sleeping together. Have I called Shelly recently to say I'm sorry?"

"Yes. And you didn't need to. She understands the name of the game. And she trusts us. So, I will talk to Trace if you want to see if I can be on your detail." He paused. "Not for anything nefarious."

That made me laugh. "Because whoever works with me might end up in a song, right?"

Jason rolled his eyes. "No, because the paparazzi and everyone involved is going to say that. You've never written me, and I know you won't. And even if you did, I'd get a kick out of it. Shelly would play it for hours on end, and with the baby coming, that'd be nice."

"Shelly's pregnant?"

"Yes. You want to see the sonogram?"

Bethany clapped her hands. "I haven't seen the sonogram yet. Show me, show me."

He pulled out his phone and showed us the sonogram, and I sighed looking at the little black-and-white piece of rice.

"Oh, they're so pretty."

"It's because they look like Shelly, right?" Jason asked, wagging his brows.

Jason was hot as heck, something that the paparazzi and media had loved to point out during the week that they assumed we were sleeping together.

The song that I released afterward had nothing to do with him, but they twisted the narrative so it would match with their theories.

"Anyway, you'll need detail when you go out and visit anyone. If you do. You know the rules."

Carrie Ann Ryan

"I do, and I'm grateful. Although you might end up as a rebound or a second-chance song. Watch out."

"Hey, anything to make my wife smile will work. You guys have fun, and we'll be around when you need us."

He closed the door behind him, and I sighed. "At least he gets it."

Bethany raised a brow. "Who does the world think you're dating now? Fictionally or not?"

"No one, and that worries me because you know they're all waiting for my next breakup song."

Bethany sighed. "Just relax, have dinner with us tonight, okay? At the house."

"I'd love that. And yes, I do need to relax. Thanks for having me here."

"Don't worry. I'm always here. And just so you know, there's construction on the north end. So beware of the area. Though it hasn't been bothering guests yet."

"What's it going to be?"

"A spa. Finally."

My eyes widened. "The Wilders are putting in a spa?"

"I know. I'm shocked. But we have the space for it, and the need. We've had to send people over to another spa, and they're booked to capacity too. We're happy to finally add it."

"Well, I'm going to be your first customer."

16

"No, you're going to have to stand in line with us girls. And maybe some of the Wilders. Elliot and Everett are both chomping at the bit."

"None of the other Wilders? I would assume Elijah would enjoy that."

"Him too. Not all of the Wilders are in the mood for dipping in a mineral spring."

I had a feeling that East wasn't one of them, but I wasn't going to bring him up. Mostly because if I did, it would just stress me out and maybe make Bethany wonder why I would mention him at all.

Bethany said goodbye, and I stood on the porch, notebook in hand, breathing in the air that I knew would probably make my nose itchy later.

Damn allergies.

I needed to write, to sing, to focus.

And I would do that.

Because this was my home for now.

I'd had homes all over the world, because my job let me.

But I didn't have a place to go home to.

I just wanted something different.

I wanted what Bethany had. A family.

"Didn't know you'd be here," a familiar gruff voice said from the right of me, and I turned, the hairs on the back of my neck standing on end.

I *loved* that voice.

I *hated* that voice.

"Just for a few days. To visit Bethany."

And not you.

I hadn't realized how cool my voice had gotten until he raised a brow.

"Okay then. I'm off to work. Hope you're not recording anything in there because I'm about to use hammers and saws."

"Don't worry. I'm not writing a song. At least not now," I said pointedly.

He raised a brow and looked around as if he were searching for something, then shrugged and made his way toward the construction area.

I ignored the way that his green eyes sparkled. His dark hair looked messy, as if he'd run his hands through it over and over again.

His beard was longer than before, and it would probably be rough against my skin, but I ignored that shiver.

I ignored everything about him.

He wasn't mine.

I had promised myself a long time ago, multiple songs ago, that I was never going to fall in love again.

Love hurt, and inspired me to write a song that changed it all.

And I wasn't about to write another.

Chapter Two

East

The letter in my hands burned. Seared flesh from ink on paper. I ignored it. It wasn't a physical pain, but I would've preferred it had been. It seared my soul and my memory. I crushed the letter, tossing it in the bin next to my desk, and shook my head.

"There's no bringing him back. There's nothing for me to do."

I repeated that mantra over and over until I finally grabbed my phone, shoved it in my pocket, and made my way outside, slamming the door behind me, annoyed with myself. I had a list a mile long to do, and I wasn't in the mood to do any of it. I needed to get on it though, or it would never get done.

"East!" Elliot called out as he bounced towards me.

He always fucking bounced. It didn't usually bother me too much because I was used to the way Elliot had a constant surplus of energy, but on my grumpier days, I wanted to throttle him. Of course, that was on me, not on him. Usually.

"What? I have to go meet the crew and I'm not in the mood."

"When are you ever in the mood?" Elliot asked, shaking his head. "But seriously, we have a family meeting at noon."

"Are you kidding me? We just had one two days ago. How many fucking family meetings do we need when we all work at the same place, and most of us live here?"

"I don't know what crawled up your ass and died, but shit it out and just be in the conference room at noon."

I winced at that visual. "Well, now I'm just thinking about a roach making a home up somebody's ass, and I just died a little inside."

Elliot shuddered. "Why did you have to get so descriptive?"

"You started it."

We looked at each other and burst out laughing. Some of the tension that was riding me since I had seen Lark the day before finally began to ease. I didn't know what it was about her. No, that was a lie. I knew some of it. She was fucking hot and smart, and I knew exactly what she felt like beneath me as I plunged into her.

And that wasn't something that I would ever feel again. So I needed to get over myself and whatever annoyance I had with her. The further I stayed away from her, the better for both of us.

"What's this meeting about?" Elliot paused, and I narrowed my eyes at him. "What is it?"

"Maybe nothing. I have a few phone calls to make, but just be there, okay? And don't shoot the messenger."

I glared at my brother. He was the youngest of us all, except for Eliza, our only sister. He and I were also the only two that hadn't settled down with someone permanently.

Each of our brothers had finally succumbed to the end of bachelorhood.

Eli had gone and married our wedding planner. Now they were parents to a little girl and didn't even live on-site anymore. Evan married his ex-wife, something that confounded me, considering I thought the two should have just stayed married in the first place. But no, they made mistakes, fixed them, and somehow figured matrimony was the way to go. Now they were parents to twins and lived on-site in a place that they had built.

Everett, my twin brother, was only here half the time these days because he spent the other half with his fiancée, Bethany. She was an Oscar Award-winning actress, and considering that they wanted to spend as much time with each other as possible before their wedding, which was coming up pretty damn soon, we rarely saw Everett. But most of his job was on the computer anyway, so he was able to work remotely. It was just weird not having him here.

Which was odd, considering that none of us had lived near one another for years. When we were on active duty, we hadn't been stationed together. None of us had the same specialty, and had gone in at different times, except for Everett and me. In the end, when the world had literally destroyed us, and only one of us had made it through our twenty, we came together.

It had originally been Eli's idea to make this resort and winery work. Our eldest brother liked fixing things. And he hadn't been able to help our sister. No, she had helped herself, had dug her way out of the hell of becoming a widow. But now she was happily married, a mom, and living up in Colorado.

The rest of us lived outside San Antonio, becoming innkeepers and wedding hosts.

It didn't make any fucking sense, but it seemed to be working.

The winery, of course, was a surprise, but Evan and Elijah ran it well. Elijah was dating our tasting room and wine club manager, the two of them so fucking happy it was nauseating. And that was another one down, again, just leaving Elliot and me.

"I need to go. You okay?" Elliot asked, bringing me out of my thoughts.

"I'm fine. I just need to go work on the new site. The contractor's already there, and I have to be in charge, apparently."

Elliot winced. "You're damn good at what you do."

"I'm a handyman. Not a contractor."

"You have a contracting license. And you are a licensed electrician and plumber. You have it all. I don't know how you were able to do all that, but you have it all."

"I needed the skills in order to fix this place. Something's always breaking down."

"Yes, please scream that for the guests. They'll love to know that everything's falling down around them."

Elliot was the major event planner and seasonal detail man. It was nothing like what he had done in the military, but none of us were doing what we had done in the military. Elliot was damn good at rearranging everything to make sure people had the best time that they could, so they came back, gave great reviews, and had more people come.

I would rather not see people at all since I didn't like

anybody, but them staying here meant that we had an income. That meant we had roofs over our heads.

At one point, those roofs had all been on the property, but now we were all moving on. I was just grateful that Elijah and Maddie had decided to stay on-site instead of buying their own place.

We were running out of family members that lived here, and I didn't know how I felt about that.

"See you at noon," I growled as Elliot's phone buzzed, and my brother waved me off before working on probably the thousandth thing he had done that morning, on his fifth cup of coffee.

That probably wasn't great for him.

I passed a few of the guests and nodded my head in hello. That was all they were going to get, and they were lucky I didn't growl. I didn't like it here all the time. I didn't know what was wrong with me. I just fucking hated change, and everything just seemed to change these days without warning. Everybody was getting married, having babies, and settling down in ways that made me uncomfortable. It had taken me forever to figure out how to be a civilian and change my outlook and life completely after getting out of the military. And by the time I had found my footing, Eli got married. And then the next one and the next one.

We even had a damn celebrity wedding coming up

—*again*—on our property. People I saw in movies and on TV were going to be rubbing elbows with people like me. Covered in dirt and not in the mood to be there.

It didn't make any damn sense, and sometimes I just wanted everything to slow down so I could keep up.

And didn't that make me sound like an old fucking man rather than someone in their thirties? But my back ached, my head ached, and while I knew most of it was because I had been thrown into more than a few walls and out of buildings, it was also just because I was damn tired.

Out of the corner of my eye, blond hair made me blink, and I narrowed my gaze.

No, I wasn't going to think about her. But of course, she was here.

She was always fucking here.

But she kept moving, earphones in place, as she bounced her head to some song.

And then Lark turned the corner. I didn't see her anymore, and I did my best to push her out of my mind. Because I didn't want to think about her. I couldn't.

But I was just damn tired of wondering exactly how we had gotten here.

And the thing was, it wasn't going to get any better soon. Because eventually, Elijah would get married, and Elliot would probably find someone, and then people would just keep moving away.

At some point, we'd have to ship in our cousins in order to fill the spaces that my brothers had left. Honestly, that wasn't too bad of an idea. I knew that my cousins were thinking about relocating, and we made a pretty picture, but that would just be more change. And I was so tired of change.

I went to the construction site, nodded at my team members, and went to speak with our contractor.

We were building a spa. A spa with mineral pools and solariums and random fucking things that didn't make any sense to me. If you want a dip to relax, then go to the lake, or jump in the pool. We had both. But no, they were going to want to hit themselves with branches or some shit, inhale lavender, or whatever. I knew that Elliot was working with the manager and director, and they were going to focus on what services we were going to have—including the juice bar. A fucking juice bar. There was even going to be an infinity pool or some shit, and while the contractor, architect, and I had worked on figuring it all out, it still didn't make any sense to me.

But it was the next phase. We were a destination. People came for the wine, for relaxation, for weddings, and events, and now they were going to come for a massage.

They used to be able to come up to specific rooms in the inn, but now it was going to be a whole experience. I still had no idea how this had become our fate, but here we were.

And I had a feeling that our next project—the restaurant that was going to be Kendall's pet project—was going to give me a headache as well.

By the time noon rolled around I was starving, and I remembered I had skipped breakfast. I was a damn idiot, but it was my fault.

I went through the back entrance of the inn, not wanting to deal with guests, and waved at Naomi and Amos. Amos worked for the winery, and Naomi was our innkeeper. They were growling at one another, but I ignored it. I did not want to get into whatever the hell was going on there.

I nodded at the few guests who saw me, knowing I was covered in dust and looked like hell.

The family wanted me at this meeting? They were just going to have to look at me and deal with it.

I had a scowl on my face as I walked into the board-room, covered in dirt, and starving.

Kendall raised a brow and pointed towards the table on the sideboard. "There're sandwiches there. Eat something. And don't growl."

I raised a brow at my sister-in-law. "Evan's teaching you how to deal with me, is he?"

"Somebody has to. Now get over yourself."

"I love you, too."

Evan just glared at me. "Don't be mean to my wife."

"You growl more than I do."

"I'm married and a dad. What of it?"

I flipped him off and went to the side table, where I picked a roast beef sandwich with cheese, onion, and horseradish. My mouth watered as the scent hit me.

I ate one in two big bites before I made my way over to the table, another sandwich in hand.

"At least use a damn plate," Elliot muttered. I rolled my eyes, tracked back to the food table, and made myself a plate with more food on it, grabbed a drink, and a napkin just so Elliot wouldn't yell at me again.

"Well, now that East the Grouch is here, we can begin," Eli muttered.

"I don't live in a damn trash can. But I do say fuck as much as I think Oscar should."

"Oscar the Grouch does not say the word *fuck*," Bethany said with a sigh.

It was nice to see her here, though I wouldn't tell her that. All of the women married into the family, or at least dating into the family, were here. It was a family meeting after all, and even though Maddie and Elijah weren't married, she had been a Wilder in every way that counted long before they started dating.

"Okay, why am I here?" I asked, before I took a big bite of my sandwich.

Everyone paused and looked at each other, and I swore under my breath.

This had to do with Lark. It had to. She wasn't at this meeting, though she shouldn't have been. She wasn't a Wilder, wasn't dating anyone.

And no one knew we had slept together the last time she was here. No one knew that I had treated her like shit because things had gotten too real, and I didn't want to be with a pretty princess. No one knew that she had walked away, then written a damn song that hit number one on the charts.

Or maybe they did know. And maybe that was why I was here, eating my last meal.

"Francesca quit."

I blinked, trying to recognize the name. And then the food in my stomach turned to lead, and I set down my half-eaten sandwich. "Are you fucking kidding me? First it was the chefs, and the wedding planners, now we just lost our spa director? What the hell. What did you do?" I glared at Elliot.

Elliot raised his hands. "If anything, it was something that you did."

"Are you fucking kidding me?

"He doesn't actually mean that," Eli said with a sigh.

"Nobody did anything. She quit because she got a better offer in Connecticut."

"Connecticut? She wants to live up north where it gets cold?"

"You used to live in the Northeast," Eli said, and I glared at him. The other man used to growl more than I did, and his attitude was always off the charts. But now he was happy and settled and bugged me to no end.

"That has nothing to do with it. She's really moving to Connecticut?"

"She met a man," Alexis said with a sigh before she rubbed her temples. "And he lives up there."

"Where the hell did she meet him?"

Everyone looked at each other, and I cursed. "Let me guess, he was here for a wedding, they met on property, and now she's in love and has decided to ruin our lives."

"Honestly, pretty much," Elliot said with a sigh. "I don't know what the hell we're going to do, but I'm working on it. I swear," Elliot said. "But until then, we're going to need your help."

Everyone turned to me, and I quickly shook my head. "Oh no. No fucking way. I'm not a spa director. I have no idea what the hell I'm supposed to do with that stuff. The only type of facial I know about doesn't actually belong in a spa."

Kendall's lips twitched as everyone else rolled their eyes or growled under their breath.

"Please, not while I'm eating," Maddie said, speaking up for the first time. "And that's not it. We're all doing a thousand things already, and with the wedding coming up it's a lot."

"Sorry," Bethany said.

I shook my head, feeling like an ass. "You just got back from whatever press tour you've had to do and you have to go on set soon. I get it. It's about time that you guys have this wedding, and it's going to be a pain in the ass no matter what. But that's not on you," I added quickly when the others glared at me.

"That's the sweetest thing you've ever said to me," Bethany said, fluttering her eyelashes. I rolled my eyes. I liked Bethany. Hell, I liked all the women that were married into the family, but that didn't mean I wanted to deal with whatever they were going to throw in my lap.

"I'm already dealing with the construction, and then breaking ground on the next restaurant."

Kendall clapped her hands, and then winced. "Sorry. I'm just really excited about that."

"I'm excited about it too, mostly because I like food. But all that means I don't have time, either."

"It won't be too much, and we actually have a plan."

From Maddie's tone, I wasn't going to be in the mood to hear it.

"What is it?"

"Lark's parents used to run a spa, and she worked at it before she really took off in the music business," Bethany began, and I tuned out the rest of what she was saying.

Because I really didn't want to hear it.

It was like a wind tunnel in my head, and I tried to tamp down on the headache.

Every time I got stressed it did this, so I took a deep breath and ignored it.

I had PTSD. Yes, I knew about it. Yes, I dealt with it.

But it wasn't going to matter right now. Because I knew why it was happening.

In this instant.

Because of Lark.

Because it was always fucking about Lark.

"No. There's no fucking way."

"She'll help."

I raised a brow as I glared at Bethany. "And what am I supposed to do, have her run a spa when she's out making millions or whatever?"

Bethany blinked at me, and I realized I had a little more venom in my voice than I should. But hell, what was I supposed to say?

I didn't want to work with Lark. I didn't want to see

her again. But I couldn't stop this. Couldn't make her understand.

"But we're going to hire a new person, right?"

"We are," Eli put in, bringing everything back to focus. "But in the meantime, we've actually already spoken to Lark, and she's willing to help. But you're point on this. I'm sorry. We thought we had a handle on it, but we don't. You don't have to learn how to give a massage, or even deal with the business parts. We've got that. But we need input. That was what Francesca was doing. So, now Lark's going to help. And you're going to have to let her."

At that, my headache raged back, and I knew today was only going to get worse from here.

Chapter Three

Lark

"I thought you were the path to my future, but in the end, you were the fork in the road I refused to take."
    "Violet Memories" written by Lark Thornbird

I joined the call with my team, and sent a quick text off to my producer while listening to the rest of the team.

Me: *I'm working. Hard as I can. Or hardly working. You know the joke.*

Jeffrey: *You know I love when you work. If you need us out there let us know.*

Me: *I'm still at the drafting stages. But when it's time to put it together, I'll meet you guys somewhere.*

Jeffrey: *I have this studio at home. It's all yours, like always.*

I smiled, loving the way that Jeffrey and I worked. It wasn't how many recorded, with set booking times and lots of moving parts. Mine was a little different because I wrote my own songs, and I needed to find the inspiration to make that happen.

But I needed to get my ass moving, since I only had three or four songs for this record. Only I wasn't sure that they were ready yet. Once I took this needed vacation, I would get together with my band and the music would flow. I wrote the lyrics, and much of the music. My producer worked his magic. My band had been with me for the past three albums, and we worked well together. We toured together. They also worked on other artists' albums when they weren't working on mine. I was Lark Thornbird. But they weren't beholden to me, just like I wasn't beholden to them. As long as we got our work done, that was all that mattered.

Me: *I have a few songs that I can send over soon. But I'm still thinking.*

Jeffrey: *It hasn't taken you this long before. Are you okay?*

I really wish he hadn't put it like that. Just because he was right didn't mean I wanted to face it.

Me: *I'm fine. I just wanted to make it right. You know. All the pressure.*

Jeffrey: *Yes, seven Grammy nominations and two wins against some stiff competition is always going to be a lot.*

I snorted.

Me: *I got New Artist of the Year that year even though I wasn't a new artist. I was just new to them.*

I rolled my eyes because all of my records had hit platinum. Every single one. And yet it wasn't until this latest one that the Grammys had actually seen me as a new artist. It didn't make any sense to me. As long as I was new to them, hitting the airways they wanted, suddenly I was worth it.

Me: *Well one day we'll get Album and Record of the Year. Though Song of the Year is my dream.*

It was the Songwriter's Grammy for a reason, and that's who I was. Or at least, who I wanted to be if I could get the damn words out of my head and onto paper.

Jeffrey: *You got Pop Artist of the Year. Although your country fans love you.*

I rolled my eyes because I was a pop artist. I was also a little more singer-songwriter than many of the pop artists out there, so some of my albums could be classified as country because I liked the guitar. It really just depended on my mood.

But that wasn't here nor there, because I wasn't putting out a country album this time. I liked country albums. But I wanted something a little softer.

Me: *I'm thinking of making this one more of a story. One where they have to listen to the whole album from beginning to end.*

Jeffrey: *A narrative? Damn straight, you could do it. Who's it going to be about?*

That's when I winced. Because I loved Jeffrey and he usually got it. Except sometimes he didn't. He didn't think I slept around with every man and woman in my vicinity. He didn't think I wrote every song about a specific person. But he also assumed that many of my songs were about real people, and he wouldn't take no for an answer.

I didn't want to start this conversation again. Sometimes it felt like that was all I did. So I sucked in a breath, and answered.

Me: *You'll just have to wait and see.*

Jeffrey: *That's my girl. Send me over what you have. Unless that's not for the album?*

I looked at my partially full notebook, and then at the empty one sitting next to it.

Me: *I'm not there yet. I'll get there.*

Jeffrey: *We need to strike when the iron's hot. But you also deserve this break. So find your balance.*

I rolled my eyes because he could talk in two different

directions all day, and it wouldn't help me figure out what I needed to do any faster.

I said my goodbyes and went back to my notebook, wondering what I was supposed to do.

I loved this job. I loved writing and performing. It was as if I was a different person on stage, where the world could hear what was in my soul, even though I was still trying to figure it out.

Yet, most of the time I didn't feel like I knew what I was doing.

I hadn't loved the way that I wanted to love. I hadn't loved the way I thought I could write.

Because while I did put parts of myself and my past into my work, I didn't write about people that I loved. Not in that way.

Because the one time I had gotten close to that, the world hated me for it.

Or perhaps I just hated myself.

Because he was gone, he wasn't coming back, and the world didn't let me forget that.

So maybe I wouldn't do a narrative album. Because the only person I could think to write about I promised I never would.

I should center it on myself, on my growth, only I knew I needed to grow first. That was the whole point.

This album would not be about East. There would not be a single *wild* pun in any title.

Someone knocked at the cabin door and I pulled up the screen on my phone, grateful for that sense of security, and then hopped up quickly to open the door for Bethany.

She stood there, eyes bright.

"There's my best friend."

I threw my arms around her, hugged her tightly, as we danced on the porch, laughing.

"It's so good to see you."

"I mean, it's only been like twelve hours."

I rolled my eyes and hugged her again. "So, what's the plan for this evening?"

"Wine, of course. And girl talk. Maddie is setting up the employee lounge for us."

"I love that place. Although I do think I spend more time drinking in the employee lounge than I do in any other part of the retreat."

"I know, right? There're so many beautiful areas for wine at the winery and the inn itself, and soon at the spa."

"And yet we always pick the lounge with its decently sized windows, dim lighting, and comfy chairs."

"It's the best."

"Is there really going to be alcohol at the spa?"

"Of course. I mean, you're going to have to detox something from your pores." Bethany's eyes brightened.

"That does remind me, there's something we need to talk about."

"Okay, that doesn't give me good vibes," I said as I picked up my things and locked the door behind me. We hopped in the golf cart and headed across the property to the winery.

I loved this place, the rolling hills, the large oak trees that twisted in their odd knobby and gnarled ways. It was a gorgeous area, and the Wilders were taking good care of it. While building the spa, they were making sure it was ecologically sound, and using a lot of reclaimed materials. Other than the restaurant, most of their property was going to stay as it was. The plants that were put in were native to the area and helped soak in water when needed, which helped prevent flash flooding. They knew what they were doing, and if they didn't know, they either learned or brought in somebody that did. I loved how they worked together, how they were so careful.

We made our way into the winery, and I was grateful for the privacy. While most people knew that Bethany was on and off the site, nobody knew I was here yet—at least online. At least the paparazzi hadn't caught on yet. Of course, Bethany's bodyguard Trace had helped set up the new security and things were locked down tightly, keeping us safe. I appreciated that, and Bethany and everyone else did, too.

The Wilders had a few incidents in the past, giving them reasons to increase their security. It was a large part of their budget now, and I knew it was stressful for them, but they were keeping each other, and their guests, safe. And you couldn't really put a price tag on that. Not with everything they had seen.

The girls were already there, making Bethany and me the last to arrive, and I went around hugging them tightly.

"You're here," Kendall said as she hugged me.

"You smell like sugar cookies."

"I was baking some with the twins earlier. Evan wanted some and I was in the mood to bake."

"You guys make my heart hurt in the best way," I said, wondering if I could put that into a lyric.

"I see the way your mind is working. Please, if you do write a song about me baking, let me know." She preened as she said it, and I rolled my eyes, before Maddie put a glass of sparkling rosé in my hand.

"Try this. It's something new."

My mouth watered. "This looks amazing."

"Do the sniff test and everything. I taught you well."

I laughed, then did everything that she told me before I took a sip. The bubbles burst on my tongue, the taste tart and sweet. I swallowed and grinned. "This is my new favorite."

"Oh good. We're venturing into new things, and while

we're not going to have this batch every year because sometimes the grapes just aren't there, this year is going to be a blast."

She went on to talk more about grapes, as Alexis came forward and handed me a little side charcuterie plate.

I nibbled and laughed with my friends, and everything just felt right.

Naomi came in after a moment, her short hair pulled back from her face.

"Hey there, everything okay?" Alexis asked and Naomi nodded.

"I'm great. Just a little tired. I don't think I'm able to stay, I just wanted to come and say hello and thank you guys for inviting me."

I waved at Naomi, who took a bite of cheese for herself, and grinned. "I love cheese. It's one of my favorite food groups."

"Amen," Kendall and Alexis said at the same time, and I just sat back and watched; people watching was one of my favorite things.

When Naomi left to go deal with a few other things on her list, Alexis cleared her throat.

"Lark, I know you're busy writing a new album and trying to relax, but I have a favor."

I stiffened, wondering why they were all staring at me.

It wasn't as if they knew. They couldn't, right? I

hadn't told them about East. And I wouldn't. That was just between us, and something that would never happen again. Even though I really wanted it to happen again.

Damn it.

"What can I do?" I asked, hoping my voice sounded casual even though I was anything but.

"Our director for the spa quit. Walked away from their contract, and is paying a penalty for it. They're not going to be getting a reference from us either."

I looked between them, frowning.

"That's terrible. But how can I help?"

"Well," Bethany began, and I snorted.

"I mean, I don't think I'll be that much help. Do you want me to find you someone? I can ask my previous contacts."

"We actually have a couple people we are talking to, but that would be wonderful," Kendall put in. "But also, can you look over what we have?"

I blinked. "I write songs for a living. I perform music. I have no idea what goes into a business like that."

"You run your own business, thank you very much," Bethany put in. "So don't tell me that you don't know how to run a business."

I waved her off. "Because it's my company. I know what I'm doing with that. But, of course, I can look it over.

I can also ask my parents. They run something similar in size to what you're doing, I think."

"That would be wonderful. Honestly, we just need someone to stand by East for these couple of weeks while we find someone new. So he doesn't growl and push everyone away," Alexis said with a laugh.

I froze as everyone began talking at once, coming up with different scenarios about how East could push people away with just his growl alone.

Work with East? Intimately? On things that neither one of us knew exactly how to work with? Well, good. That wasn't going to go badly at all.

"Wait. East is in charge of it? Now that your person left?"

"Francesca left us in the lurch, and while we have a contractor that actually does the building, East is the Wilder in charge of it. He calls himself a handyman, but that's a lie," Alexis said with an eye roll.

"He's brilliant at what he does, but there are those nitpicky things that we could normally help with, though we're all working on one hundred different things. Especially with the wedding coming up," Bethany put in quickly.

I let out a breath. "So, you need me to, what, hold his hand so he doesn't blow up at the contractor? That seems a little dangerous."

"It's not dangerous," Kendall said, her eyes wide. "He would never hurt you."

Not in the way that they thought.

I held up my hands in protest. "I never thought he would. He's not violent." I winced. "I'm sorry."

I didn't know exactly who I was saying that to, since practically everyone in this room had gone through something horrific of their own.

"We would love any help you can provide with those connections. Eli's working on it from his end. And your parents could help so much. But also, we just need someone who has seen these things before. Can make sure that East is guided while we look for a new Francesca."

I bit my lip, knowing I only had one answer. These women, and the men that they were connected to, had become part of my family. I didn't know how exactly that had happened, because I had my friends on the road, my friends in the industry, and I had my family at home, though I didn't get to see them as often as I wanted. But Bethany was it for me. She was mine. And I would do anything for her.

Even work with a man that didn't want me anywhere near him.

"I'll make sure he doesn't yell at people. I guess."

"That's not what you need to do, or maybe that is exactly what you need to do," Kendall said with a laugh.

"I'll get you those numbers and talk to my parents. And I guess I will work alongside East. Maybe it'll jar some lyrics loose for me."

Bethany frowned. "You're still having trouble?"

I winced. "It's annoying. I sort of know where I want to go with this album, but nothing's coming to me right now, so maybe I need to do something else. Maybe I could be the new spa director. Even though I am not qualified at all, and only worked at one as a kid."

"You still have much more experience than me," Alexis said with a laugh. "And, while I can't help you with song lyrics, there is love all around us, and weddings galore. Maybe that will help too."

"And you never know, there could be a groomsman just waiting to be your inspiration," Maddie added with a laugh, and I just rolled my eyes and sipped my wine.

I hadn't meant to blurt out that I couldn't write, and while Bethany still gave me looks of worry, the others didn't. Because maybe they thought that all writers had writers' block like this. And they did.

But I didn't. This was so unlike me.

I needed to just get through it. And if the Wilders needed me to help them, I would.

When we left, I walked back, foregoing the golf cart. The air felt good on my skin, the crickets and cicadas working their magic so it seemed like I was in a storm of sound rather than out in the Hill Country. The path was lit perfectly, so I felt safe and all I had to do was just keep walking and make my way to my cabin. I was full, happy, and had only had one glass of wine, so I wasn't even buzzed.

Tomorrow I would have to go to East and see if there was anything I could do.

Not that he was going to let me.

I turned the corner and ran smack dab into a hard chest. My fingers dug in, and I tried to pull back, embarrassed as hell that I hadn't looked where I was going.

And at the familiar voice cursing, I looked up and saw him.

East Wilder glared down at me, his eyes narrowed, not looking any happier to see me than he had before.

Chapter Four

East

My hands reached out instinctively and I gripped her shoulders. My heart raced, though it shouldn't. I knew who this was; it wasn't like before. This wasn't the darkness, there was nobody screaming. I wasn't back there. My friends weren't dying, and I was safe.

Instead, an irrational anger slid over me.

"Are you kidding me? What the hell do you think you're doing walking around alone?"

Lark's eyes widened before she glared at me. "Are you joking?"

"You shouldn't be out alone. You could get hurt at night like this."

Again, I knew it was irrational, but it wasn't like I could stop myself. Not when anything could have happened to her.

"I'm safe on your property. Trace built a team to make sure of it. And there's lights everywhere on this path. It's not like I walked off into the middle of a field where a coyote or a snake or an armadillo could get me."

"First off, an armadillo isn't going to hurt you."

"You don't know that. Have you seen their beady little eyes?"

"I've seen their eyes, they aren't beady. And if anything, I thought you'd be more afraid of an opossum than you would an armadillo."

"Opossums are cute. And they protect you by not being a carrier for bad diseases that can be transmitted to humans. And they get rid of unwanted pests. They can prevent Lyme disease by eating ticks, and they have a resistance to snake venom. They're adorable, and they play dead. I just think that's unique."

I let go of her, realizing I was still holding her, my thumb sliding along her shoulder.

I hoped to hell she didn't notice, but I knew she probably did. She noticed too much, and I hated that. I ran my hands through my hair. "Why do you know so much about opossums?"

"I don't know. I saw a video on the internet. And armadillos are scarier. They have that armor."

"Next you're going to tell me you're scared of a turtle."

"Have you seen a snapping turtle?"

"We don't have those here, and we are now getting off-track."

"Again though, not off the path. I'm safe here. The team is protecting me. All of us. In fact, I just saw Jason walking back to his guard station. He knew where I was going, and that I was getting home safely. We're in the light. It's fine."

I narrowed my gaze. "But you aren't just anyone."

I wasn't sure why I had said that. I shouldn't have, it was too much.

It was hard to think when it came to her. It was always hard to think when it came to her.

"Sure. You say that, and then you ignore me. You yell at me every time you see me. We had sex, East. You don't have to hate me because of it."

She said the last part quietly, just in case anyone was listening.

I wanted to growl, to scream. "What the hell is wrong with you?"

"What the hell is wrong with me? No, I'm done. If you don't want me here, you're just going to have to deal with it. I'm trying to give you your space, trying not to be in your general vicinity, but I can't help it that every time I turn around, you're right there."

"This is my place. My home. What do you expect me to do?"

She threw her hands up in the air. "Excuse me? I just don't understand you."

"I said that you're not just anyone, and you got snarky. What the hell do you mean by that?"

"You know exactly what I mean by that."

"Come with me. We're going to talk."

"I'm not going anywhere with you."

"You know damn well that we need to just get this out."

She raised her chin, and it was as if I had no idea who I was anymore. I wasn't the kind of person who wanted to talk. But Lark was just pissing me off, and I needed to get this over with.

"We're closer to my cabin. Come on."

"So you can yell at me in private? No, thank you."

"I'm not going to yell." I practically yelled the words.

She raised a single brow, and I snarled.

I held out my hand. She looked at it and scoffed.

"Are you kidding me right now?"

"Five minutes."

"Why should I?"

"Because we need to talk this out before the rest of the

family realizes that all we do is yell at each other. And I'm not in the mood to deal with my brothers and sisters-in-law annoying the fuck out of me. What about you?"

She stared at me but didn't put her hand in mine. Instead, she turned and began to walk towards my cabin. My cabin was closer than hers, that's the only reason I had mentioned it. Not because I wanted her in my space.

I unlocked the door and stepped aside so she could walk in first.

With a sigh she stepped past the threshold. I reached over her, belatedly remembering that I needed to turn on a light for her.

My arm brushed her shoulder, both of us freezing at the action, and I swallowed hard, doing my best not to react. It was damn hard not to react when it came to her.

It was always so damn hard.

Hell, I was hard, but I wasn't going to think about that, that wasn't what this was about.

"Okay, what did you want to talk about?" she asked, and I sighed.

"What do you think I wanted to talk about?"

"No, we're not going to do that. You're going to tell me what you want to talk about. Why you felt the need to bring me in here in the middle of the night, right before bed, so you can what, yell at me?"

"I don't want to fucking yell at you. We just need to

talk about this. And I don't even know who the hell I am right now. Wanting to talk? Who am I."

She laughed then, a sweet laugh that did things to me.

"Honestly I'm a little shocked too. You want to talk. About what? Us? There is no us. We made it very clear that there isn't an us. I'm fine with that. You were an asshole, and I get it. You don't like me. But we had sex, and we're just going to have to deal with the fact that we fell into each other."

"We fell into each other because I found you hot and you found me hot."

She blinked at me, before she threw her head back and laughed.

"That's what you're going to go with. We were hot for each other, so I guess us accidentally falling into bed and having hot sweaty sex is totally fine."

"What do you want me to say, Lark?"

"How about the truth?"

"Fine. I wanted you. There. We were hot for each other just like we said, and we both went into that situation knowing it was going to be one time. Your best friend is marrying my brother in a few short weeks. We just have to deal with this."

"I know. You want to deal with it then we're dealing with it."

"And it's fine. We slept together and it's over. I don't know what else you want me to say about it."

"I don't know what else I want to say about it either. I'm damn tired of wanting you." I hadn't meant to say that, but there was no taking back the words.

"You still want me?" she asked, eyes wide.

"Of course, I do. You're beautiful and you know it."

"That's not the same as wanting me. I've had a lot of people tell me I'm beautiful."

"Yes, because I want to hear about those other people."

She threw her hands up in the air. "I don't know why you hate me."

"I don't hate you."

"It sure as hell feels like it."

I sighed and moved forward. I didn't even realize I was doing it until I was touching her face, my fingers brushing along her cheek.

"I don't hate you. I don't know you."

"You sure knew me well enough when you were inside me."

I snorted. "Yeah. I did. But you knew me too."

"East. Don't look at me like that. You know that's a very bad idea. We hate each other."

"Do we? I don't think I can hate you, Lark. Not when I want you this much."

What the hell was I doing? I hadn't had a drink that night—I wasn't drunk, I wasn't exhausted. And yet I was making a fucking mistake. But that was the problem when it came to Lark. All I did was make mistakes.

From the first moment I saw her, I had wanted her. I knew that I couldn't have her.

"I can't do this," I whispered.

"Can't do what? Yell at me? Ignore me? Make me feel like I don't know what I'm doing? Because you're damn good at it."

"I don't want to want you."

"Same here."

At the venom in her voice, there was only one thing I could do. I leaned down and crushed my mouth to hers.

We froze as we both tried to come to terms with exactly what we were doing, and then we moved. She slid her arms up my chest, digging her fingernails deep into my shirt, and I grunted, sliding my hands down her hips, gripping hard, knowing I might leave a bruise.

"I hate you."

"Same here," she snarled, before I was kissing her again, pressing her back to the couch. I was rough, far too fucking rough, and it didn't matter. I tugged at her hair, pulling her head to the side so I could suck on her neck. She moaned, sliding her hands around me as she slid her fingers up my shirt. She scraped at my skin, and I thrust against her, grinding as I continued licking and sucking and tasting. I needed to stop this. Neither one of us needed this. All it was going to do was complicate things and make us hate each other even more, but I didn't fucking care right then. I was addicted and she was my drug and all that mattered was that I had to be inside her. Had to taste her and to feel her and never let go.

It didn't matter that I would hate her even more after this, hate the fact that she made me feel, hate the fact that she didn't. Hated the fact that she didn't want me for more than this. But that was fine. I didn't need anything else.

We were nothing to each other, and I damn well knew that.

The more that I pretended we could be something else, the more that I let myself fall into those hot dreams, the more it would hurt in the end. Because we were nothing for each other. And yet we were everything in this moment.

We tore at each other, grinding and breathing in heavy pants. I pulled up her shirt, groaning at the look of her lace-covered breasts.

"You're so fucking beautiful. But you're even fucking hotter naked."

"So many words not being yelled at me. I'm shocked. I didn't know you could speak without yelling."

"You know what would be better? With you on your knees and my cock down your throat. Maybe that would shut you up."

She grinned as she knelt; I pushed her down a little harder.

She let out a soft oof and I smiled, unzipping my pants, pulling my hard cock out of my pants, and pressing the tip of my dick to her lips.

"Are you ready for me? I've wanted to see this for far too long."

I'd imagined this in every dream, and I knew I should stop, that this might be too rough for her, but as her eyes lightened and she put her hands on my hips, I thought, *maybe not*. And then she opened her mouth, and I slid deep into her. She groaned around my cock when I reached the back of her throat. She gagged, then swallowed a bit more, relaxing her throat as I kept going.

She was so hot on her knees, just in her bra and her jeans, with my cock in her mouth.

I wanted to keep going, to fuck her face hard. But then she began to move, and she was the one in control. I didn't know if I could take it, but I started to thrust, wrapping her hair around my fist. She held on, her fingernails digging into my thighs.

She kept making those wet gagging sounds but humming along me. If she wanted me to stop I would, I wouldn't force her, God, of course I wouldn't. But she kept moving her head, once again proving she was in control, and it was all I could do not to come down that pretty throat of hers.

When my balls tightened and I was nearly ready to come, I pulled out of her and tugged at her shoulders.

Before she could say anything, I crushed my mouth again to those swollen lips, my hard cock pinned between us.

She was so beautiful, so soft. I should stop. But I wasn't going to.

I hated what she did, what she represented. But I wasn't going to stop. Not unless she wanted me to. And she didn't want me to.

She tugged at my shirt, so I pulled it off and then reached around and undid her bra. The lace fell between us, her breasts more than a handful, her nipples pert, pink, and perfect for my mouth. I leaned down and sucked one between my lips, biting down gently at first, and then a little bit harder. She moaned and rubbed her thighs together against me. I grinned before I slid my hand over her jeans and cupped her.

"I can feel you all hot and ready. I haven't even touched you there, but I know you're wet, aching for my cock. Are you ready for me, baby?"

"I hate you."

"You say the sweetest things. But I fucking hate you too."

I didn't know if I was telling the truth, but I didn't care. I wanted to hate her. Because it would make things so much easier.

She was so warm against me, and I needed to be inside her. I undid the button of her jeans and slid my hand underneath her panties.

She was wet, already soaking my hand. I grinned.

"I knew it. You're wet for me, just from sucking my cock. Does fighting turn you on?"

"Just shut up and fuck me already."

"I already did, and I will do it again."

"You're so full of yourself. You yell at me for no reason, of course I hate you. But fuck me anyway."

I snorted. "Whatever you say, princess."

"I'm not a princess," she snapped.

"Really? You're the pop princess that everybody loves. And yet you're here, slumming with me."

"Fuck you."

"I'll be fucking you soon." I slid my finger deep inside her and her pussy clenched around me, as if waiting for me.

"So eager."

"You're an asshole."

"Yeah. I am. And yet, I don't care. You're a liar. And I don't care either."

"Stop it."

"Do you want me to stop right now?" I asked, freezing.

"I didn't mean that. Keep fucking me, I meant just stop yelling at me. Stop that."

I slowly pumped my finger in and out of her, and then added a second. She moaned, rocking against my hand.

"I can do that. You want me to end this? I'll do that, too."

"Don't you fucking stop."

"That's exactly what I wanted to hear." Then I slid my thumb over her clit, rubbing small circles, and she came, arching her back, her breasts bouncing, her hips rotating on my hand.

I nearly came right then and there, spurting all over her stomach, but I held back, barely. Without thought, I shucked off her jeans, and then mine, scrambling for a condom, knowing that if I wasn't careful, I was going to slide right into her unprotected, and we would hate each other even more.

When she took the condom from me, ripped it open with her teeth, and slid it down my cock, it was the hottest thing I'd ever seen.

Sweet and pampered little pop princess knew exactly

what to do with a condom.

Didn't want to think about that because it wasn't my business. She could fuck anyone she wanted. And I *shouldn't* care. Only, I was just a little possessive. And yet, it didn't matter. Because I was fucking her now, and in the end she'd walk away, write another damn song, and fuck someone else. I couldn't blame her for that; it wasn't my problem. She wasn't my problem. She could do whatever she wanted, and I couldn't judge her for that. I could just judge her for the fact that she had lied to me.

And the fact that I wasn't going to be able to keep her.

I pushed those thoughts from my mind, gripped her hips, and lifted her on the edge of the couch.

"You ready?"

"Again, with the talking."

"I liked you better with my dick in your mouth. You shut up then, didn't you?"

"And you only shut up when I'm riding your face, and yet you didn't do that, did you?"

"Next time."

She rolled her eyes. "Like there's going to be a next time."

I slammed into her then, both of us groaning. She let out a slight scream, and I froze, waiting for her to accommodate me.

She was always so sweet, soft-spoken, gentle with

others. Oh she could command a stage, could rock the roof off for hours, but was still the sweet one. The pretty pop princess.

And yet with me she was the dirty-talking rocker who came on my cock, her legs wrapped around my waist.

I didn't know what that said about me, but it was the hottest thing I'd ever seen. I must be dreaming, because this didn't seem real.

I rode her, both of us sweat-slick, as I tried to come to terms with what was happening. It didn't make any sense.

When she came again, I followed her, hating myself just as much as I hated her.

I stood there, balls deep inside her, her legs wrapped around my waist, as we both panted, fighting to catch our breath.

"Well. That was interesting."

"I'm not a liar."

And with that, I pulled out of her, leaving her sitting at the edge of the couch. I just stared.

"Really? I was just deep inside you, and you're going to lie again?"

"I already told you to fuck yourself, but I guess I need to say it again. Because I'm not a liar."

"Then why did our song hit number one?" I snapped, and she paled, and I knew I was right.

Damn it.

Chapter Five

Lark

"I hate the thought of looking at you, yet the moment I close my eyes I know you've always been there. And there's nothing left of me to hold onto. Nothing left for me to bear."

"Mirror" written by Lark Thornbird

I was so angry, but I didn't know if it was at myself or at him. Because I had just done the one thing I told myself I wouldn't do. I'd fucked East Wilder.

"Are you serious right now? *Are you serious?*"

"Of course, I'm serious. I heard your song, we all did. And I know who it's about."

"You're such an egotistical asshole," I snarled as I

jumped off the couch and reached for my clothes. "Go take care of the condom so I can yell at you."

"Oh, that's sweet pillow-talk."

"I don't really care what you think right now. But we're going to clear the air, and I can't do it with your dick all out like that."

He looked between us before he threw his hands up in the air and went to the bathroom to go take care of the condom. He'd grabbed his clothes along the way, so I stood there, getting dressed, wondering why I hated myself so much.

"I heard the song. And you hit number one. Good for you. But it was the one thing I asked you not to do."

"First off, you asked that after you came in me the first time. And you were so rude about it, I was shocked. I don't know why you would've thought I would have ever done that."

"It's what you do. You're an artist," he said, such disdain in the word. I hated him in that moment. I despised him.

"Okay, we're going to get a few things straight. I write songs for a living. I am a writer. Get over yourself. It's not like I antagonize and judge everything that you build."

"That has nothing to do with it. They aren't even comparable."

"Maybe. But I don't know why you have your panties

in such a twist about what I do. And for the record? You don't have to listen to the paparazzi and the media. I don't write songs about real people."

"Are you serious? You're known for writing songs about your exes."

"Because that's what the media thinks." I threw my hands up in the air. "I don't write songs about real people, and newsflash, my new single, I wrote *months* before I ever met you. You and I slept together because we wanted to. Because there was chemistry between us, and maybe that was enough. But then you left me sitting there, in the cold, feeling like I had done something wrong for wanting to sleep with you even though you're the one who started it. I don't know if you understand how my industry works, but in the few months between us meeting and the song coming out, there is a lot that takes place. It's not like a record can just be put out overnight. It takes time, careful planning. It's not something that I write on a Monday, produce on a Tuesday, and release on Friday. You're so full of yourself, you are literally that other song about being so vain. I did not write that song about you. I'm never going to write a song about you."

That last part might be a lie, but I didn't tell him that. My soul desperately craved to write that song, the one that was whispering sweet words to me, but I wouldn't.

And even if I put those words to paper, I would never release it. Because that was my promise to him.

"Are you serious right now? You expect me to believe that?"

"You have to believe me because it's such a stupid thing to lie about. I have only written about one person in my life. Everything else is maybe glimpses of people, but it's never out like that. That song that just hit number one? It was about an idea about a person. It wasn't a real relationship. I haven't even been in a real relationship in forever. And that might make me sound desperate, but how am I supposed to be in that type of relationship when every single time they're so worried that I'm going to write a song about them, that the paparazzi is going to invade their privacy, that they don't even want to be with me?"

"It wasn't about me." He kept saying that as if he were trying to make it make sense, but now the two of us were on the same page because nothing made sense.

"Such an ego. No wonder we fight more than we fuck."

His lips twitched. "I like it when you say the word fuck, it sounds so odd coming out of that sweet little mouth of yours."

"I can't help but be both. I am that sweet person that people think I am, and I have the mouth. I like sex. There's nothing wrong with liking sex, but I don't have sex with every person that I meet. I don't write songs about every person that I meet. Or even every person that I've ever been on a date with."

There was silence between us. I wasn't sure what I was supposed to say, what I was supposed to do. Because I didn't open up like this, but it hurt that he kept blaming me for something that wasn't my fault. That wasn't even about him. There was something else going on here, but I didn't know how to fix it.

"Who was the one person?" he asked, his voice low. There was an odd pain in it, and I didn't know where it came from.

"Nobody knows that. Not really. And I don't know if you deserve to know that." My hands itched, my heart ached. But I was done. So done.

He ran his hands through his hair and gestured towards the kitchen. "Do you want some water? I could use some water."

I looked down at my hands. "Yeah, I could use some water."

I followed him to the kitchen, where he filled two glasses of water from the fridge inside.

"I'm not good at this. I've been in a shit mood since I could remember." He handed me the glass of water. I sipped slowly as he practically chugged his, then went for another. We stood there in the kitchen, him with his pants unbuttoned but zipped up, his shirt inside out. I probably didn't look much better, sure that I had sex hair, swollen lips, and a beard burn. I just wanted to go home. I wanted to write again without feeling this. To not feel this pity, this pain, but that was what made a good writer, wasn't it? You used your pain and your trauma to try to figure out how to write.

Maybe that was all bullshit.

"That one song? The song that people love the most, yet didn't win any awards. That's the song you want to hear about?"

He leaned against the counter and stared at me. "If you want to tell me. Or I can walk you back to your cabin and we don't have to talk again. I'm done yelling, I'm done being angry."

"So, you believe me?" I asked dryly.

"I'm an asshole. I'm in a shit mood and I took it out on you."

"Why?"

He stared at me, and I knew he wanted to say something, but he didn't. Instead, he just shrugged, and I knew it wasn't my right to ask anymore. We didn't owe each other anything. Maybe we owed each other a little more respect than we had given one another. But he had been in a shit mood and taken it out on me, but then again I had done the same. I was rude to him when I wasn't to others; I wasn't kind, I yelled and I cursed more than normal.

I didn't know what it was about him, but I didn't hate him. Even though I said I did, I just hated how I acted around him.

"My song 'Mirror.' The one that people still write about on message boards and social media about it touching them in some way, it was my one song about a real person. They think it's about a past lover, but there's someone else in that mirror."

He frowned. "I know that one, but I don't know the lyrics."

I stared at him, and he shrugged again.

"I know your work, Lark. I did before I met you, and I like it. I didn't like the fact that I thought the new one was about me. But that is selfish. You're right, egocentric. I'm trying to get over myself. I'm not very good at it."

He gave a self-deprecating laugh. I wanted to join him, but instead I swallowed the rest of my water and set the empty glass on the table. Then I rubbed my suddenly clammy hands on my jeans and stared at him.

"I was nineteen when I wrote 'Mirror.' Six months after my birthday. I was already on the road then, you see, on my first tour. I was opening for another artist that I loved. My first album was out and I was doing pretty well."

He set his glass down, his face darkening. "Lark, you don't have to tell me this. It isn't my right to know."

"No. It's your right. Because I'm making it. Because I never tell anyone this. Bethany knows, and I don't know, I just feel like telling you. So let me do that, okay? Please?"

He nodded. "Okay."

"My bassist was a drug addict, but I didn't realize it at the time. No one did. He was really good at hiding it. He was friendly and happy and really talented. He was on my first album, my first tour, and people loved him." I stared at him then, and maybe he could read it in my eyes, because his jaw tightened.

He knew. I didn't have to say the words, but I was going to. Because I needed to.

"He OD'ed at the end of that tour, because he loved drugs more than he loved his bass, more than he loved anything else. Addiction is a disease, I understand that. And maybe to anyone else I should hate addiction, hate how it took him from the world. And I should find a way to help. I would help anyone I could. But with him? I don't know. I don't think I was that helpful. Maybe I am bitter. Maybe I'm not the sweet person that people think I am." I let out a breath and I looked him square in the eyes, my throat dry, but my words steady. "Everyone misses him and says he was a talent. But I just saw a man who tried to force himself on me. More than once."

70

East didn't move forward, didn't reach out to touch me. He didn't know if I would welcome a touch just then, instead his jaw tightened and he let out a low breath, his chest moving deeply. His hands fisted, one on the counter, one by his side, and maybe that anger soothed me so I could keep going. Because nobody knew this. If they had, the media circus would've intensified.

"I wrote healing into my lyrics, and I keep trying to. I keep trying to write about love and happiness so it makes sense. So much so that people think the songs are about real people. And maybe that's an amazing and wonderful compliment, but right now it just gives me this over-whelming urge to scream. Because everybody needs to link every single lyric I have to a person and a place or memory."

"Lark."

"No. I'm okay. I know it sounds trite, but I've had amazing therapy, and I talked it over with my family, and Bethany. I've slept with people. I've slept with you."

My throat tightened and I tried to breathe, tried to think about what to say next. I never told others about this. I didn't want to. They didn't need to know, and all it would do was hurt who I portrayed to the world.

East looked at me then as if he were *looking* directly into me and figuring out who I was. He opened his mouth to say something, then closed it again. When he moved a step forward, I didn't move back. I knew this moment could change everything or nothing. "I was way too fucking rough with you. I don't want to say you should have told me, because that wasn't my right to know, but I'm sorry."

Of all things he could have said, for some reason, that was the best. I didn't know what was wrong with me in that moment, but I could finally breathe again. Damn him. And perhaps, damn me too. "No, don't apologize. I like what we have done. I would've said something if I didn't. I like it a little rough and I like you touching me, I like all of that. And I'm dealing with it. I promise you. This has nothing to do with you, other than you need to understand that I've only written about one real person, and that person wasn't even him. It was me. In the end, it was always me. So no, I didn't write a song about you. I'm not going to release a song about you. I'm not what the media portrays me as, and it hurts to think that you would believe that. But then again, everyone else does."

He huffed out a breath and moved forward. I braced, not knowing what would come next, but he just cupped my face and leaned his forehead on mine. "I'm a shit."

"You are. But I was one right back to you."

"I don't have the words to adequately say how sorry I am. Because they're trite in comparison to what you went through. I am sorry though. And I'm sorry that man is dead so I can't kick his ass."

I snorted, surprising myself that I could even laugh in this situation. I just slipped my hands around his waist, twisting my fingers along his belt loops. "I'm not good at this, you know."

"Same. And I'm sorry. For being such an asshole. You didn't deserve that."

"You didn't either."

"And I don't know where to go from here because you're here to work on your next album. And all I do is yell at you."

"I'm also here to apparently help you with the spa," I said dryly.

He laughed before he pulled back, shaking his head. "Apparently. I have no idea what I'm doing there."

"I don't either, but I have friends that do. I'll help." I paused. "For Bethany," I added quickly.

He met my gaze, and I didn't know if I was lying or if he thought I was. "For Bethany."

Then he stared off into the distance, and shrugged, as if he were trying to figure out if he was going to say what was on his mind. But that was East, he usually did. At least to me. And it was usually with a growl.

"And while you're here, if you want to keep sleeping together, we should. We're good at it."

I stared at him before I burst out laughing.

Of all things he could have said, that wasn't what I was expecting. I just bared something so personal that only a few people in my circle knew. And he hadn't hidden from me. Hadn't been so gentle to me that he'd be afraid I'd break. If anything, he was the same as always. That made me like him even more, and it twisted something deep inside me that hurt, but in the best way possible.

Because he didn't see me as broken. I was still just Lark to him.

"You want to sleep with me. While I'm here."

"Why not? Like I said, we're good at it."

I stepped back, shaking my head. "You know what, you don't tell secrets. You were so worried about me telling the world in a song about you, but I don't want the world to know what I'm doing either. You're not going to tell the world that you slept with Lark Thornbird."

"Of course, I'm not."

"So, what, friends with benefits while I'm here?"

He tilted his head. "We're friends now?"

I didn't know if he was just being an ass on purpose, or if I was supposed to be hurt by that; instead I sighed.

"Okay, enemies with benefits. How's that?"

He grinned then, making him so damn handsome it was hard to breathe. Yes, his twin brother Everett was marrying my best friend, but right then they looked so different.

And East was so damn hot, so damn intriguing.

"Enemies with benefits? I like it."

I rolled my eyes. "Fuck you," I said, knowing he liked when I said fuck.

He winked and slid his hands around me, cupping my ass. "Already did." And then he kissed me again, and I knew that night was going to be a long one.

Chapter Six

East

I had no concept of what I was supposed to do.

"We're working on the back deck area, it's going to be a long day. This is just shit work, but I'm glad that you're here."

Our contractor squeezed my shoulder, before going to the other guys.

They had me in charge of the site, but I wasn't qualified to run the whole thing. This hadn't been my job in the military, and it damn well wasn't my job now. Our contractor gave us the work, and I filled in when they needed, but also had to somehow ensure if things were correct or not.

It was a complicated business, and honestly, I didn't really want to be part of it. I didn't know how I'd ended up here. I was just a damn handyman. But now I was building buildings, not just fixing things.

I went to help lift a few loads of lumber, something that I was qualified to do.

I just had to focus so I wouldn't let my mind wander.

Especially because all I wanted to do was think about a certain woman that I shouldn't be thinking about.

I could not believe that I had even broached the subject of sleeping together. But here we were.

Both of us deciding that maybe this was exactly what we needed. Or at least wanted.

There was no way this was going to end well. In fact, it would probably blow up in our faces. Especially once the rest of the family figured out what we were doing. And they would.

My brothers knew way too much about everybody's lives.

There was no way that they wouldn't figure out that Lark and I were doing whatever it was that we were doing, and then I'd have to deal with the consequences. Not Lark. She'd be fine.

I sighed, pushing those thoughts from my mind.

I didn't need to work through anything. We were just friends who would fuck again.

I snorted. "I'm an idiot."

"What was that?" the plumber next to me said, and I shook my head.

"Nothing. Just talking to myself."

He snorted. "That doesn't sound like a sane thing to do, boss man."

I flipped him off and he laughed, and we went back to work. I worked on the spa for another hour before my phone buzzed and the rest of my day beckoned. I waved goodbye to the contractor and made my way to my work cabin.

I lived in a small cabin on the east side of the property, but I had a separate one where all of my supplies and tools were.

When we renovated the place to what we needed it to be, everybody had fallen into jobs that made sense. Jobs that used their brains, and their creativity.

I hadn't known where to fit in. I didn't like numbers. I wasn't qualified to be an accountant or CEO or anything like that. I didn't like wine, I didn't know about making wines. But my brothers did. They all fit in and learned what they didn't know.

I wasn't good enough with people to deal with them on a daily basis. Elliot had been born for that even, though he had gone a different route when he was active duty. So now, here I was, doing the only thing left to me. Using my hands.

I had a team if I needed it, others on staff that could help out. But I fixed things. If a cabin needed a new floor?

I put it in. Something electrical needed to be tweaked? I was qualified. Same with plumbing, and even putting in new windows in cabin number four last month. That's what I did. I worked my ass off, I stayed away from people, and I went through my long list that never seemed to dwindle.

Today I was working in the inn itself, as our innkeeper, Naomi, had a wobbly baseboard in the main center. The main inn itself was two buildings, they were connected with a second-floor alcove and walkway. One building held most of the rooms for people to stay in, as well as a few meeting rooms. The other building was the main entrance where Naomi did most of her work, as well as eateries and the kitchen where Kendall worked as our brilliant chef.

I entered through the back area, not wanting to scuff up the floors in the front entrance where guests were.

We were a decently high-end establishment, so people came in wearing linen suits and driving fancy-ass cars.

I didn't tend to fit in, but Lark did, as did Bethany. They had even brought us up, at least that's what my sisters-in-law said.

They brought in new clients, clients that meant more money for us so we could upgrade things and make sure we always were above the bottom line.

Naomi waved at me, her short brown hair tucked

behind her ears. "Thank you so much for coming in. It's just behind that bookshelf over there, I feel like the base-board is buckling. But maybe I'm wrong."

I held back a curse, because guests were milling around the front entrance, looking at the delicate library books or playing chess in the front window.

"Damn it. It better not be a leak."

Naomi winced. "We're just going to think happy thoughts."

"Okay, you keep doing that." I paused. "Is Amos off today?" I asked, though I didn't know why I was curi-ous. I had a feeling that my brothers were rubbing off on me.

Naomi blushed. "I don't know what you're talking about. And if you want me to not ask about a certain person I saw you walking with last night, you won't ask me."

I froze, meeting her gaze. "Understood."

"Exactly. Now, that's where the buckle is."

"I've got it. Thanks."

Of course someone had seen us. It wasn't like we were hiding in the dark. No, we'd been right underneath a light. At least it was Naomi and not one of my family members. Yet.

I nodded at a guest who smiled at me and went back to her book. Then I went to the bookshelf and moved it forward a little. It was heavy as hell, and I grunted, looking down at the floor.

I didn't see an obvious buckle, but Naomi had noticed something.

"Do you need help?" a deep voice said from beside me. I froze, before almost turning and punching out without thinking. I hated being startled, I hated anyone coming up from behind. I didn't normally leave my back unguarded like that, but there hadn't been an option in this small space. Then the owner of the voice registered and I didn't know how to react.

"Here, let me help you move it to the side a bit more. It's heavy with all these books."

"I got it," I bit out.

"I'm sure you do. But here, you don't have to do it all by yourself."

He helped me and I nodded in thanks, noticing that the baseboard had popped up. Probably just because the place was still settling. I didn't see any damage. It looked like whenever we put in the shelf itself, the workers had knocked into it. I quickly pressed it back down and took note. Whenever everybody was out, I'd replace it. It was a quick fix.

I hated the fact that corners had been cut.

My back still to the other man, I cleared my throat as I moved back. I stood up and I heard the man behind me shuffle back. I turned and saw exactly who I thought it had been. Goosebumps pebbled over my flesh, it was as if I was being thrown back in time. I didn't want to think about this. I couldn't.

I couldn't breathe. Fuck. I couldn't breathe.

"You know, I thought it was you," Lawrence said as he stared at me. He slid his hands into his pockets and rolled back onto his heels.

I stared at the other man, but I wasn't really seeing him. I was hearing the screams, seeing the fire, feeling it on my face.

Lawrence didn't have any scars on his face or his neck or arms. Nothing visible. But I knew they were on his back and his legs. I knew he had gouges in his chest from his time being a POW. They had taken him. Tortured him. But he found a way out. We had gotten him back.

It wasn't *we*. I hadn't been able to do anything for him.

I blinked, my breath choppy, and Lawrence cursed under his breath.

"I'm sorry. I didn't mean to... I just..."

He kept trailing off. I swallowed hard, bile coating my tongue.

"What are you doing here?" I asked as I willed myself to breathe. Only I couldn't breathe.

"I'm staying here. With my wife. Anniversary. I figured this was your place. I didn't know how I was supposed to tell you I would be here. That I wanted to talk to you. Didn't really even know this was you fixing this until I saw you."

Lawrence kept speaking, and yet all I could hear was a buzzing in my ears, my palms going damp, everything getting a little hazy.

The headache attacked me, and it was hard for me to breathe. Hard for me to do anything.

"East?"

"I've got to go," I growled out, then I shoved past him, being careful not to hurt him.

Because I wouldn't hurt him again.

I left the bookshelf out in the middle of the walkway, and I didn't care. I just needed to breathe. So I kept moving, kept going.

Leaving Lawrence behind.

Just like before. I thought he was dead and I hadn't been able to save him. Almost everyone else had died and I thought Lawrence died right along with them. I had kept going. I hadn't had a choice then. But I didn't have one now, either. Because I couldn't breathe.

I made my way behind the building, slamming the back door open and sucking in mouthfuls of air and yet I couldn't get enough oxygen.

My chest squeezed, tightening, and I bent over as I threw up. All the water that I had earlier poured out of me, whatever was left of my breakfast following right along.

I hoped to hell there were no guests around, because this wasn't something they needed to see. But there was nothing I could do about that now.

"What the hell? East? Are you okay?"

Elliot came towards me, his hand outstretched. I pulled away from him without thinking. I looked up to see the hurt cross over his face, but then he narrowed his gaze, and put his hand on my shoulder.

"Talk to me."

"I'm fine."

"You're not fine. Are you sick? Did something happen? What's wrong?"

I didn't tell him. I didn't tell anyone. I'd never told my brothers what happened. Oh, they knew that we had been attacked, that most of my team died—I couldn't hide that. But they didn't know details.

Elliot ran his hands over my back to try to soothe me, but I needed to get away. He didn't need to see this. Elliot had been through his own hell, like the rest of our brothers had. I didn't need to put my issues on them. I was strong enough to handle this on my own.

I didn't need to hurt them.

"Can you go fix the bookshelf? I might have fucked it up. I've got to go."

Elliot stared at me and was quiet for a moment before he nodded. "Of course I can. You only need to ask. I've got you."

I knew he wasn't talking about the fucking bookshelf. But I wasn't going to ask. I wasn't going to do anything. I nodded tightly and left. I ran like the fires of hell were chasing me.

I left Lawrence behind again, and now I was leaving Elliot behind. Because that's what I was damn good at.

I made my way to the tree line, leaning against one of the tall oaks, trying to suck in gulps of air and yet feeling like I wasn't getting any.

Nothing was there.

I didn't realize it was going to affect me like this. It hadn't in so long.

I knew I had PTSD. You didn't go through what I had without it. My therapist had said I had it and gave me ways to deal with it. But there was no dealing with it when my past slapped me right in the face.

Lawrence had come back. He had survived, but it was my fault that he had been left behind. So I wasn't going to stand there and look at him. I didn't deserve that.

When a small hand touched my back between my shoulder blades, I whirled, fists ready. Lark froze, eyes wide, as she stood there, one hand outstretched, the other at her side. I'd almost hit her. I'd almost hit Lark for daring to touch me. For coming up from behind me just like Lawrence had.

I was usually better at this. I usually protected myself better.

And yet I'd almost hit her.

"I'm sorry. Damn it. I'm so sorry. But don't fucking come up behind me like that. I could have hurt you."

I was yelling the words, and I didn't care. Why couldn't I think? Everything hurt and I was going to throw up again.

Lark did the bravest thing I had ever seen her do. She put her hand on my chest, right over my heart. Could she feel it race? I could hear it beat so rapidly in my ears I was afraid it was going to burst into a thousand jagged shards.

"East? You didn't hurt me. I startled you. But you didn't punch out. You didn't lash out."

"I can't, I can't breathe."

"Okay. Do you need me to call someone?"

I shook my head, trying to keep up with my own thoughts even though they were going in a thousand different directions.

"Are you sure?"

I nodded, and then my knees went weak. I fell right there on the ground, my knee slamming into the packed dirt.

Lark let out a sharp gasp, and then she was on her

knees next to me, wrapping her arms around my shoulders.

"I need to call for help."

"I'll be fine," I bit out. "I just need to catch my breath. There's nothing they can do anyway."

Lark looked me directly in the eyes, and I wanted to reach out to her, to touch her, to taste her. Because maybe her taste would push away the demons.

It wouldn't. But maybe, maybe I could pretend.

She pushed my hair back from my face and nodded. "Okay. I'm here though. And you can't push me away."

I wasn't sure I was strong enough to do so anyway. When she held me, I closed my eyes and let the shaking come. My teeth rattled, my shoulders quaked, but I was breathing. I was letting her hold me.

I didn't want her to see me like this. I didn't want anyone to see me like this. I couldn't stop it though. I let her hold me, and I hated myself with each passing moment.

Lawrence had almost died, nearly everyone else *had* died. I wasn't strong enough to face it. Nor was I strong enough to stand on my own two feet. Instead, I let Lark hold me. A small part of me knew I needed it.

The rest of me hated every ounce of myself for letting it come to this.

Chapter Seven

Lark

"I never asked to fall, yet with one look, I knew I didn't have a choice. What am I without you? What am I with you? What am I in between?"
    "Falling" written by Lark Thornbird

I missed the days when my job was just writing music. When all I had to do was let my imagination flow, and the words and notes would come easily. They might not always have been perfect, and needed heavy revisions, but it was a start.

And then I got my first record deal, and all of the complications that came from that meant that I was constantly working on the next thing. I had to work with my agent, my producers, and other songwriters who wanted to work with me. There were fittings and photos and shoots and publicity and interviews and countless other demands on my time. I had choreography; even though I didn't dance during any of my shows, I still needed to know where to go. I had to make sure I wasn't just standing in front of my mic with a guitar in my hands and not moving. It was all just so confusing, and it took hours of my day.

Even though I was technically on a sort of vacation, away from the rest of the world, I was still having to do everything that I could from this small cabin. That morning I had gotten up, gone for a jog, and worked with my trainer.

There was a music awards show coming up soon that I had to make sure I was ready for, and that meant there would be practice, and working with my band. They wanted to come out here so we could make sure we were ready for that. I liked my band. I liked working with them and they would be out here soon; we were constantly working on the next thing.

It wasn't just writing the music, that had to be the foundation, but it wasn't my only job anymore.

That's what worried me—the music wasn't coming as easily as it used to. All I wanted to do was anything else so that way music could make sense again. I hated feeling like I wasn't doing anything right.

Perhaps that was just on me. Perhaps this was just my problem.

I needed to figure out what the hell I was doing with East Wilder. Because I had no idea what I was doing.

I knew that my time of being alone out here was running short, and that would be fine. I had a job to do. People relied on me. I had a team, just like Bethany did. It was just weird to think that my job wasn't writing anymore, even though the one song that kept coming to mind was one I couldn't write.

With my guitar on my lap, me sitting cross-legged on the floor, I closed my eyes, and let the song come.

They say the hardest part is taking the fall.

But they never tell you the risk comes by saying nothing at all.

I promised myself I'd never let him see.

Then the world lied to both of us, and I can't make him believe.

I kept singing, humming along to a harmony that I would eventually nail down.

The words poured out of me, and I quickly wrote them down, using the notebook that was just for this.

When I finished, an odd sense of relief filled me. I looked down at the notebook and cursed.

Here I was, doing the one thing I told myself I wouldn't. The one thing I promised him I wouldn't.

I quickly shoved the notebook to the bottom of my bag, unable to throw it away or burn it, but unable to look at it.

I promised I wouldn't write about him. That was the goal. Not to write about East. He had been so mad at me, had practically threatened me when he thought I had in the first place. I wasn't going to make a liar out of either of us.

Why was he the only person I could think about when it came to songs?

I needed to work on my new album. There were so many other things I needed to do. And yet here I was, only thinking about East. There was seriously something wrong with me. I knew that though. There had to be something wrong with me if I was thinking that I was going to allow myself to continue to have an enemies with benefits relationship with him, like we had joked.

Yet all I wanted to do was touch him again, to feel him again.

I needed to change that.

Only, I didn't think I would be able to.

Sighing, I put my guitar away, and rolled my shoulders back.

I had a few meetings later I couldn't get out of and I

didn't want to. Like I said, people relied on me, and I wasn't going to be a flaky artist that nobody could get ahold of.

I put my phone in my pocket, my headphones on, and figured I would go for a walk. It was a nice enough day, only a few clouds in the sky, and fresh air would help.

Maybe somebody needed my help. Something that had nothing to do with East or writing.

I hadn't been much help when it came to the spa yet. But I had asked my parents for any advice and sent the email over to Eli rather than East, and he hadn't batted an eye. Maybe everybody saw the animosity. But I didn't think they had seen anything else. Maybe we're good enough at hiding it. Whatever *it* was.

I couldn't get the sight of East breaking down in my arms out of my memory. Something had happened. Something terrible I couldn't fix for him. But the fact that he had been vulnerable at all, had leaned on me, did something.

That's where those words had come from, words I shouldn't have written down.

I could not fall for East Wilder. I could not want him for anything more than the time we had together now.

It would break me. I knew that.

I knew what happened when you yearned, when you believed. East wasn't for me. I had to remember that.

"Hey, there you are!" Bethany said as she skipped towards me. Literally skipped.

She was so in love and happy, and I was not at all jealous.

"Hi. I thought you would be in meetings all morning," I said as I opened my arms and hugged my best friend.

She kissed the top of my head, and we both laughed. "I thought about it. But now that I did a couple hours of meetings with executives for the next movie, I'm taking a break. A long needed one."

"Good. You deserve it."

"I'm glad you feel that way. Because I'm exhausted. Between this and the wedding planning, it's a lot."

"I'm being the worst maid of honor, you know. You haven't asked for help with anything. Not even your bachelorette party."

She waved me off. "The Wilders have it all down. Seriously. And we already talked about the bachelorette party. It's just us hanging out. You don't need to do anything."

"I'm going to figure out something."

"You being here when I know you have a thousand things to do is more than enough."

"Still, I'm going to go talk with the girls. We'll plan something."

"I'm just happy to be marrying the love of my life."

"Honestly, I'm ecstatic for you to marry the love of your life, too."

And I wasn't jealous at all.

Well, maybe a little. But it had nothing to do with her.

"I do have a couple of questions about the wedding, though, maybe we can go over them over dinner? Everett and I would love to have you at the cabin."

"Your cabin is bigger than my house in LA," I said with a laugh.

"That's just because you refuse to buy anything bigger than a closet there."

"It is so expensive to live in LA. I only do it because my friends are there, and it's easier for work."

"You make damn good money; you don't need to live in a closet anymore. Plus, you need better security."

I paused, remembering everything that Bethany had gone through. I had gone through my own hell, too. Only mine was from someone I trusted. Then again, so had she. Just in different ways. She was right. I needed to be smarter about my security. Only it meant I would have to do something new. Take a chance.

I wasn't sure if I was ready for that.

"I'll try. I don't know, I just feel like everything's moving at a thousand miles per hour around me, and I can't keep up."

"Well, you're not alone. We've got you. And Everett

and I can help you find a good house. Hell, your manager can help you find a great house. She's great at that."

"She's been asking me to move for a while now. And you're right, my neighborhood is wonderful, but it's not gated."

"And you don't have the type of security that you really need." Bethany paused. "And honestly, you know that Trace has been trying to get you out of that place forever."

I snorted, thinking of her bodyguard and security team manager. "It seems like forever doesn't it?"

"Just think about it, we're here when you need us."

"I like the fact that you're a *we*. Makes me smile."

"Me too. I can't believe that this is my life." She hugged me tightly, and I agreed to dinner later.

I turned the corner, the sun beating on my face. Others milled about, but nobody really noticed me. I was grateful for that. I was in a zipped-up hoodie and leggings, and didn't really look like me, which was the goal. To be comfortable and inconspicuous.

When I looked up, I saw the man from the day before. The one East had moved away from, a scowl on his face.

I didn't recognize him, but East had, so I thought about turning the corner or turning around. Only he met my gaze, and started to head towards me briskly.

Caught, I braced myself. Jason and my security team

weren't near me, but I knew I was in shouting distance of anybody that could help. We were on property, so I was allowed to be on my own, I didn't have to have a body-guard at my side every day, but I regretted it just then.

"Ma'am?" he asked, in a deep voice that reminded me of East.

I was still an LA and East Coast girl enough that hearing the word "ma'am" always made me feel weird. I was in my twenties, I wasn't a *ma'am* yet, but we were in Texas where it is a sign of respect. Hearing "miss" was a little more degrading here, at least according to my friends.

"Hello, can I help you?"

The man in front of me stuffed his hands in his pockets as if he were afraid he was being intimidating. He was big, wide and muscled, just like East. So yes, he was intimidating.

I didn't know what I was supposed to do.

"I saw East talking to you yesterday, and I...well, I left you be because it wasn't my place, but are you friends with him?"

It wasn't my place to say yes or no. If East didn't want to talk with this man, I shouldn't either. Although it was odd that he was asking me about East, it was usually the other way around. People usually tried to talk with people that Bethany and I had spoken with in the past in order to get to us. It was part of being celebrities, and I didn't like this side of it. I didn't like the idea that perhaps somebody wanted to hurt East, and I was their way in.

"I'm sorry, who are you?" I asked, not knowing what else to say.

He pulled his hand out of his pocket and slid it through his hair.

"I'm sorry. I'm Lawrence. Well, I...worked with East."

The way he said that, with a pause before "worked," made me think that he meant the military.

"Were you stationed with him?" I asked. I wasn't a military kid. I didn't know all the lingo. But I knew enough. At least from being friends with the Wilders.

Lawrence looked relieved. "Yes. We were friends, well, until bad things happened. I don't need to bore you with that, and I don't think it's my place to tell you everything that happened over there. But East and I were friends. I just want to talk to him. And I know it probably hurts him for me to be here, and I don't want that. But, I don't know, maybe it's not right for me to ask you if you can talk with him and see if he'll just listen to me, but I don't know what else to do."

Emotions rolled inside me because I didn't know what to do either. I wanted East to be okay. I wanted this man to tell me what had happened, but it also wasn't his place and we both seemed to know that.

I was so curious, I wanted to know what had happened. Wanted to know why East didn't want to talk to this man, and why these two seemed to share pain.

But it wasn't my place. Only, I wanted it to be. There was something about East that called me to him, but I knew I needed to push that away. He wasn't mine. He would never be. What we had was only for the moment, and it wasn't my right to want more.

"I'm sorry. I don't really know you, and I don't know if it's my place to talk to him on your behalf, you know? I can ask him, but I can't make any promises."

His eyes brightened as he smiled at me, as if a weight had been lifted off his shoulders. I felt like an asshole. Because again, I couldn't make promises. And I felt like standing in the middle like this I was just going to end up hurting them both. I didn't know what happened between these two. What happened overseas. I knew that he—like his brothers—had gotten hurt. But I didn't know details, because he hadn't told me. Because that wasn't who we were.

I had to ignore that pain. That odd sense that maybe I had done something wrong.

"Thank you. He's welcome to ignore me, to walk away. But I have to try. I'm sorry for putting you in the middle."

"I'll just say you were looking for him. I'm sorry I can't do more."

"Don't be. Just, thank you. Seriously, thank you."

Lawrence walked away, and I stood there rubbing my temples.

"What the hell were you two talking about?" East asked, and I whirled, having not noticed he was there.

"What?"

"Lawrence. Did he tell you? Did he tell you what happened? Or did you go up to him and ask? You couldn't just leave well enough alone, could you? You had to be nosy. You couldn't just let me be."

Hurt, I took a step back. "That's not what happened at all. He came up to me."

"And, what, you couldn't just walk away? You just had to know? I leave for one second, and this is what happens. No. Fuck this." He whirled, stomping away, leaving me standing there as people walked by, wide-eyed. Someone even took a photo, and I knew that would probably be on social media later, because they probably knew exactly who I was.

Lark Thornbird fighting with a new boyfriend again. All alone and left behind.

I didn't like feeling like I had just made another mistake, and I hadn't. I hadn't done anything wrong. I had no idea what the hell I was supposed to do. I hadn't done what I had always told myself I would do—stand up for myself. Instead, I stood there like an idiot. I wouldn't do it again. I couldn't.

I was done.

Why did thinking that hurt even more?

Chapter Eight

East

I was an idiot. I knew that, my brothers knew that, and yet I couldn't stop.

I hated what I said to her, how I yelled. It wasn't her fault. I knew that.

"East?"

That familiar voice froze me in my tracks.

I didn't realize she would be here. That she'd want to be here. Or maybe she was here just to yell at me—I would deserve it.

"Yeah?" I asked, not bothering to look around. I needed to get back to work, and pulling out sidewalk and changing the direction of a path wasn't something that was going to be easy. The fact that we had to do this at all was ridiculous, but we weren't the ones that put in this path to begin with.

"East. Will you just look at me?"

"Don't know if I should," I said, shrugging as I looked at the path in front of me. "There're things for me to do. And every time I'm near you these days, I either want to put my hands on you, or I screw things up by being an idiot."

"What are you doing?" Lark asked.

I sighed, leaning on my shovel and turning around to see Lark standing there.

It had been a day since I yelled at her, since I had seen her talking to Lawrence and I had blown up before she could even say anything.

I was practically screaming at her in the middle of our place of business, in front of my home, and she should have hit me. She should have shoved at me or screamed or done something other than just stand there because I had scared her.

I was the problem. Me. And I needed to fix it.

"What's wrong, East?" Lark asked and pushed her blond hair from her face, the wind hitting it just right so it billowed. She wore brown leather leggings of some sort with pockets at the side, and a sports bra with a running tank on top under an unzipped hoodie.

She looked like she was out for a run, and sweat glistened over her chest, over her stomach. At least the sliver of skin I could see beneath the tank.

"Why do you have a shovel out here? I thought you'd be working on the spa."

I shrugged, grateful she didn't want to talk about the day before, but knowing I needed to bring it up. But at least this conversation could have a bit of humor.

"The contractor is working on the spa, and I'm working on this." I gestured towards the paved path that wound around the west side of the property. "Not as many people use this because we have more than a few walking paths and these were farther between cabins and the main wedding venue area, but enough that a problem had arisen."

I snorted at my joke, but Lark wouldn't get it yet.

"I don't get it," she said, frowning. "It's a good path. There aren't any cracks in it, which is impressive considering the heat you guys get here."

I nodded, before I rolled my eyes. "The path is a penis."

She blinked, hands on hips as she looked around.

"I'm sorry, what?"

"The path is a penis. Now I have to fix it."

"I know you're being a dick, but I don't understand what this means."

I blinked at her before I burst out laughing, some of the tension releasing, but not enough. Because she deserved more than my attitude, and I knew it. I just needed to be better.

"Whoever built this path before used the natural gap between the trees and the hills in order to build a path. Only when people are using their little pedometers or watches that show their tracking paths on GPS apps, it looks like a dick with very round balls. The perfect cartoon version of a dick. It's even become a meme online, so we're changing the path."

She snorted, shaking her head. "Are you serious?" She turned, narrowing her gaze at the angles of the sidewalk. "I guess I can see it. Are those the balls?" she asked, pointing.

I moved to her side and gently pointed her hand to the correct angle. That bare brush of skin sent shock waves through my body and I sucked in a breath, forcing myself to calm down.

"Over there. But yeah, it doesn't quite look like it in real life. Not unless you squint."

"Well, I guess guys do squint when they're playing with that."

I rolled my eyes. "Great. We have teenage humor going down."

"You're the one who just said going down, I can't help it. It just comes out."

"Again, that's what she said. Still though, we're going to adjust the balls I guess."

"So the length is fine, and the tip?" she asked, her eyes dancing.

I just shook my head, feeling lighter than I had in far too long. Did Lark do that? Or was it the dick jokes?

"We're going to fix it so it's not obscene. Somebody complained, and once they complain, they go to the board and the city council and then it's a whole thing. Seriously, we don't care. We're a bunch of dudes who were in the military. I think we're fine with dick jokes. And while this can be a family place, it's more of an adult-run venue. There are kids here for events, but we're not kid oriented. It shouldn't matter. But whatever, we'll do it so the city council doesn't blow a gasket, and we'll add more paths for people to walk on without hurting or damaging the environment too much."

"Well, that is a job for you I guess."

She sounded sad when she said that, so I leaned against my shovel a bit more and reached out, brushing her hair from her face. She froze, and I cursed myself. I was ruining this. Every time I thought I knew what I was doing, I messed things up.

I had to fix this.

"I'm sorry for yelling at you. For overreacting when I saw you talking to Lawrence. You can talk to whoever you want, and I know he probably approached you, because you're not the kind of person to ask other people about me. So, I'm sorry for being an asshole."

She just blinked at me, as if surprised I would ever apologize.

Again, that was on me. I was the asshole, and I hated that.

"Oh. I mean, it's not okay that you yelled, but I'm over it. I know you have things to work through, and they're not going to be worked through with me, but yeah. It's fine."

"It's not fine, but I'm working on it." That was probably a lie, but I should make it true. "I'm sorry." I leaned forward and kissed her softly on the mouth. Just a brush of lips. I couldn't help it. I needed to touch her. That was going to be a problem soon.

"Oh."

She blinked up at me, looking just as confused as I felt.

"Yeah. Oh."

"What are you doing, East?" she asked, and I leaned my forehead against hers, sighing.

"I don't know, Lark. I told you I wasn't good at this."

"I don't think you're any better than me at it. But we should stop doing this."

I froze, pain sliding through me. She couldn't mean

stopping forever, right? Though I shouldn't care. Because as soon as she left we would stop whatever the hell we were doing, but I didn't want to end it now. That was something that later me should have to worry about, not now.

Before I could say anything though, her phone buzzed.

"It's my producer. I have a meeting that I'm probably late for."

I nearly forgot she was a celebrity, a Grammy Award-winning singer-songwriter who kicked ass at everything she did. And I was just me. Standing in her way.

"Sorry. I'll let you go."

"We do need to talk, East. You know that right?"

I nodded, moving my attention to the trees behind her moving in the wind. The hundred-year-old oaks made me remember that the world was far bigger than my own problems. Even when it didn't feel like that.

"Go ahead to your meeting. I'll be working on this for a while."

Lark's eyes filled with humor for a moment, before concern edged that out. Again, my fault.

"I have to go," she said again before she leaned forward, put her hand on my chest, and sighed. "We do need to talk."

And with that, she left, leaving me standing there, wondering what the hell I was doing.

I went back to work, just breaking up some of the dirt around the pavement, planning what my next moves needed to be. I wasn't actually going to be breaking concrete today. Although it might help my mood.

"Hey," a deep voice said from beside me, and I whirled, my heart racing, and I didn't even realize that my shovel was in my hand, ready to be used as a weapon until I looked down.

"Okay, why don't you put the shovel down," Trace said as he shook his head. "Seriously. If I was a guest, you'd have some explaining to do. What the hell is going on with you, East?"

I liked Trace generally, but I didn't like him just then. He had been Bethany's bodyguard forever, and helped revamp the security here. Because of him, everybody had to check in, including those on staff and doing construction.

He was here usually when Bethany was, but sometimes he was out at her next shoot or movie set before she was set to arrive, making sure that the security was ramped up there. The guy had been traveling more often than not these days, and from the dark circles under his eyes, it was probably wearing on him.

"What are you doing here? I didn't think you'd be

here until we set up for the wedding." Which, to be fair, was coming up soon. Another Wilder down.

Of course, part of me wanted to see what Lark would look like in her dress. I couldn't help but watch her, and that was a problem.

"Things change," Trace said as he shrugged, looking around.

There was an event going on at the main house, so most of the guests were there, or in their cabins, or playing tourist down in San Antonio. Nobody was around us, except apparently Lark, and now Trace.

"What do you mean things change?"

Trace looked at me, the exhaustion in his gaze etched on his face. "I'm done doing bodyguard work."

I stared at him in shock. "Bethany fired you?" I asked.

Trace just rolled his eyes. "No, I'm just taking a new position. Bethany is here more often than not, and hell, East. I'm tired of traveling like I am. Which makes me a baby because Bethany does it more than I do, but it's not something I enjoy. So I set her up with a good team, and I'll still run it from afar, but I'm not going to be her personal bodyguard anymore."

"That's a big change. What are you going to do now? Because you're damn good at your job, Trace. Fuck, you're practically family."

Trace winced. "I know. And actually, your brothers offered me a job."

I shook my head. "They did?"

"You're probably in the email chain, and I'm sure they're going to ask you about it, it just recently happened. But I'm going to work full-time for the Wilders."

I grinned, I couldn't help it. "Seriously? You know we'd love you here. Hell, we need you here."

We'd had attacks on my family on this property, it had taken additional security, and a whole lot of courage in order for my brothers and sisters-in-law to stay on this property. Especially when they had been hurt.

"I'll be working full-time for you guys, and though I did revamp your security, I'm going to do it better. Bethany's going to be here, and now Lark is in and out. I don't know, I'm just going to work here, and do some training too. I have some plans in mind, some people I want to bring in. But I fixed the team some already; in a few weeks, I'll start doing it better."

"Well, we'll be glad to have you. Although I probably should check my email to see if they actually told me about it."

"You know they did. You Wilders don't make a decision without asking the group."

"I don't know, I'm pretty sure they'd assume I'd want

you to work with us. You know what the hell you're doing."

"I do. So that's why I want to talk about the fact that something's come up."

"What?"

"Let's start with the fact that you keep acting like a bear with a thorn in your paw, and why you yelled at Lark yesterday."

This time there was no joyful and sarcastic Trace in front of me. Instead, it was the hard-ass, the one I knew had seen some shit in his life. He could take me down in an instant. And while part of me reared back, wanting to fight—because there was no flight when it came to me—I needed to take a deep breath.

This was Trace. He was a friend. I didn't have to scream or fight.

"What the hell are you talking about?" I lied.

Trace snorted. "No, we're not going to do that. There were cameras, dammit. You were in a public space. My team, the one I set up, saw it. So, why don't we talk about the fact that you yelled at Lark for no good reason, and you should tell me exactly why I shouldn't tell Bethany right now to get your ass kicked by your brothers."

Emotions twisted inside me, and I swallowed. "They don't know?" I asked, my voice low.

"They don't. But they should. Because you guys are

thick as thieves, and I don't know why you're not telling them that something's wrong. Because you're not okay, East. If your top's blowing off that quickly from a woman just standing near you, there's something wrong. And you need to fix it. Because I'm not about to let you hurt your family. And I'm not about to let you hurt yourself."

"Fuck off. I'm fine."

"No."

"What do you want me to do? Bare my feelings to you or some shit? I'm fine. I was just having a bad day."

"You're having more and more bad days. When I first met you, you were quiet, but you didn't lash out at everyone. And now you're grumbly, you're scaring guests, and you're having panic attacks in the fucking main building."

I glared. "Cameras again?"

"And concerned friends who don't know what to do. So talk to me. You can't talk to your brothers for some reason? You won't talk to a fucking therapist? Then talk to me. Maybe I can beat it out of you."

"You could try," I warned.

"And you know I'd win. You're a bit rusty, son."

"Fine. You know I have PTSD?"

"I do. Not the details, because it's not something you wanted to talk about, but I'm not going to give you a fucking choice now. What the hell is going on?"

"Nearly every person I know who came back has

PTSD. You don't live through that without it. Some people can just breathe through it, and I thought I was doing fine. But I'm not. I just keep freaking out and my chest tightens and I don't know what the hell's going on."

"You need to talk to someone. And maybe not just me."

"I'm fine."

"Stop lying to yourself."

"What am I supposed to do?" I asked, throwing my hands up in the air. The shovel fell with a clash against the cement, but neither of us flinched. "I miss my team, okay? We were a fucking unit. And all but three of us were killed in action within a week—gunned down, blown up. I watched my friends bleed out in front of me as I tried to pull them to safety. I tried my best and they still died. And then Lawrence and another guy, another friend, went missing. They were taken. Tortured, and I couldn't save them. Another team got Lawrence out, but Franklin died. Another team saved Lawrence, because I couldn't."

Trace cursed under his breath. "I want to say I'm sorry, but I know it's not going to help. But fuck, I'm sorry."

"I'm not special. I survived, they didn't. Lawrence went through hell, and I didn't. But we weren't the only

113

ones. People every single day are going through hell, in every country, and yet I just can't get over this."

"I don't think that's something you get over, East."

"Apparently I have to, because I can't function."

"That's something you need to work on. And this friend? Is that the guy that was talking to Lark?"

Trace saw too fucking much.

"Yeah. But I don't need him to tell me he blames me. I already do. And so does Holmes."

"Holmes?" Trace asked.

"One of the other guys. He blames me. But hell, so do I."

"And you're sure about Lawrence? That he's here to blame you?"

"Of course I am. And maybe I need to stand there and take it, but I don't think I can. What kind of asshole does that make me?"

There was a slight gasp from behind me, and I turned to see Lark only a few feet away, eyes wide, phone in hand.

I turned to Trace, who looked just as surprised as me, and cursed under my breath.

Chapter Nine

East

My heart beat loudly in my ears and I sucked in a breath. Trace whistled between his teeth.

"Well, hell," Trace whispered. "I've, um, got to go."

I turned to Trace, who just gave me a tight nod. "We're going to talk later."

I waved him off, because I didn't have time to think about that, yet from the determination in Trace's eyes, I didn't think I was going to be able to avoid it for long.

"I'm sorry," Lark said briskly, hands up. She still wore her workout clothes.

"I needed to come down this path to drop something off for Bethany, and I didn't think you'd still be here. I really didn't mean to listen."

"I guess I shouldn't be speaking out in the middle of a

path if I didn't want people to hear," I grumbled. I wasn't angry at her. I couldn't be. This was my fault. I had decided to tell my truth in the middle of a path where anybody could come up.

Of course, she once again had to see me at my worst.

"I don't know what to say, even though I'm usually good with words, but, East..."

Her words trailed off and she stared at me.

"I can't, I can't do this here."

"Then maybe you should go talk with Trace again. If you need to talk about it, do it. It doesn't have to be with me. Probably shouldn't be with me."

I scowled, not knowing what she meant by that. "Come with me back to my cabin, I just, I can't fucking think."

Not waiting for her reply, I turned and went down the other path towards my cabin, grateful when I heard her footsteps follow.

I had no idea what the fuck I was supposed to do just then, but standing around in my own feelings wasn't going to fix anything.

It was a short distance to my cabin; after we got inside and closed the door, Lark let out a breath and shook her head. "I didn't mean to eavesdrop. I swear. I can't help but be in the wrong place at the wrong time."

"It's not your fucking fault," I growled.

"I didn't mean to listen."

"And I shouldn't have said what I had out there."

We were silent for a moment as I tried to come to terms with what just happened, with the fact that she now knew everything, knew why I hated myself, why I yelled and I screamed and I pushed people away.

"Do your brothers know?" she asked softly.

"They know I was hurt. That friends died. But they all lost friends. Evan lost his fucking leg."

"I don't know how you guys were able to make it through all that you did. But you're here together now. And that counts for something. Do they know the details?"

I let out a hollow laugh.

The sound of gunfire hit my ears again and I pushed it away, my palms going damp. I smelled the scent of flesh burning, hearing the screams of those who didn't make it. Then the feeling of metal against my face as the door blew in and the Humvee was knocked off the road.

I had survived the initial impact, as had three others. In the end, just two of us would walk away, only one of us unharmed. Holmes had been fine physically, but something had darkened his soul to the point I couldn't breathe. I had been hurt in more ways than one. Lawrence and Peter had been taken. When Peter died, a part of me had too.

"No, they don't know everything."

Lark brushed her fingers along my cheekbone. "Maybe you should tell them. Don't you think they, of all people, would understand?"

I whirled away and began to pace, not wanting to think about that. "Why should I burden them with this? Why would it matter what they thought about it? It shouldn't matter."

"But maybe it should, East. Your friends died."

"I don't want to talk about it."

She held up her hands. "Okay. We don't have to talk about it. I'm sorry I don't have the right words."

"Words couldn't make this better. Lawrence is here because he needs to have it out with me, and I need to be man enough to stand in front of him and let it happen."

She frowned, wringing her hands in front of her. "Are you sure that's what he wants to do?"

Why did she sound so much like Trace? Why did they think they knew Lawrence better than I did?

"Of course, that's what he's here for. And I need to just get through it. Because he deserves at least that."

"And what happens if he doesn't hate you for what you did—or what you think you did?"

I let out a hollow laugh. "It's not going to happen, so I don't even need to think about it."

"You'll take it as penance?"

"I'll take it however he needs me to take it. I don't want to talk about this anymore."

Lark just sighed. "Okay. But maybe you need to."

I narrowed my gaze at her, surprised at her tone even though I shouldn't be. She yelled at me right back. She wasn't a weakling.

"Excuse me?"

"Maybe you do need to talk about it. Because you're clearly in pain. Talk it out. Fight with your brothers, do something. Because holding it all in just makes you blurt it out at the wrong times, and you're hurting yourself and everyone else around you. Maybe you can't fix it, and maybe you shouldn't try, but maybe you should find a way to deal."

"You don't know anything about it."

"You don't think I understand pain?" She let out a hollow laugh.

I cursed, hating myself. "Lark, I—"

"So, you remembered what we talked about? What I blurted out to you? That I told you my deepest, darkest secret. The one that could rake in thousands from news organizations if you spilled it."

Anger slapped at me, but I pushed it away, knowing this wasn't about me.

"You know I would never."

"I do. I trust you and your family so much that I'm

here trying to just figure out my life. And I told you because I trust you. You don't have to trust me the same way. What happened to me, the fact that I broke at the time, and sometimes I feel like I'm still broken, yet I'm also okay. It took me a while to figure out I could even be okay. But I'm allowed to. I hope you understand that you are allowed to be okay, too. But first, you're going to have to breathe."

"I'm breathing just fine, Lark."

"Are you? Or are you barely treading water?"

"I don't know what you want me to say."

"I don't know either. But something has to change, doesn't it? You need to figure it out. Because holding it inside like you are is not helping you."

"Don't you think I know that? Don't you think I know that I'm acting like the biggest fucking idiot. But I don't know what else I'm supposed to do."

"Fine, then wallow and fight and hate yourself and hate everyone else. But I wish you would realize there's something on the other side for you. There has to be."

She stood there, looking so damn beautiful it was hard for me to breathe, and I realized she was right. I wasn't getting better. I wasn't changing things. I was barely even fixing things and that was my fucking job.

I didn't want to think about what I needed to do, what would be smart, in that moment. Instead, I took a step forward, surprising us both as her eyes widened. I reached down and touched my fingers to her lips. "I don't want to talk anymore."

She was silent for so long I knew I had probably said something wrong again. She finally sighed and closed her eyes. I nearly took a step back, knowing I had likely gone too far. It would be better for everyone if I just walked away.

"I'm so tired of talking, of words and writing songs and everything. So let's just do what we promised. Just be. You can do what you want, East. I can't stop you from living your own life, but you're right, I'm done talking."

When she went up to her tiptoes, I met her halfway and crushed my mouth to hers.

She tasted of sweetness. I knew I wasn't good enough for her, but it didn't matter because she was mine for this moment.

I tossed my phone to the side as I pulled off her jacket, needing to see her curves. Needing to see her. We would ignore our responsibilities and just be, and when I fucked her over the couch, or against the table or door, we could pretend.

"East, just fuck me already. I'm so tired of thinking."

I smiled at her, wondering how I could be so damn lucky when it came to this woman, knowing that whatever the hell was between us would end any day.

"I can do that. You and me? I can do that."

"I want you, and I'm going to have you."

Not a lie, not a promise. She continued to kiss me, and I smiled against her lips as we stripped each other down.

The couch wasn't the most comfortable thing in the cabin, but it was better than the floor. I spent most of my time fixing up everywhere else, and though my place might not be in shambles, it was still only a two-bedroom cabin, the guest bedroom more for storage. My living room was small, the couch barely bigger than a loveseat, but it didn't matter because I had her laid across the back of it, her hands on her breasts as I knelt in front of her, thighs around my shoulders.

"You're so fucking wet already."

"Do something about it. Please," she begged. I grinned in reply before I leaned down, taking her in my mouth. She was sweet and tart and I swallowed, licking and sucking at her clit. I spread her, humming along her sweet folds. Her body shook, her thighs squeezing tightly around my neck. I chuckled roughly against her, knowing my beard was scraping her inner thighs. She'd have a mark, *my* mark, and a selfish part of me relished that.

I speared her with one finger, before I pulled out and gently teased her with a second. She moaned, rocking against my face as I continued to eat her out, tasting her sweet honey.

"Come for me, come on my face, Lark. Show me exactly how tight that sweet pussy can be around my fingers."

Her legs tightened as I hummed along her, and she came in a beautiful cacophony of sound and sweetness. She was so damn beautiful, it was hard to think.

I kept sucking and licking at her, tasting her as I sucked in her orgasm, loving the beauty of it. When I stood up to press myself against her entrance, she pulled at my shoulders.

"No, not yet," she whispered.

I frowned, then remembered I needed a condom.

I cursed and searched in my pants pocket.

"Damn it, I need a condom."

"Good. You do. And I need to do something else."

She reached down and gripped my cock. I closed my eyes, willing myself not to come right then and there on her tits.

"Be careful, you're playing with fire."

She stroked up and down my shaft, gently running her thumb along the slit at the top, spreading my pre-come. "I thought I was playing with your dick."

"That too," I said, barking out a laugh. I picked her up, crushed my mouth to hers, and relished in the fact that she wrapped her legs around my waist, pinning my dick between her folds.

She rubbed against me, both of us practically shivering from each other's touches, as I carried her to the bedroom. I threw her down on the bed, laughing with her when she bounced.

"Oh yes, so suave and smooth."

"I never said I was," I growled before I reached to the bedside table to pull out a condom.

She crawled towards me, her breasts full and swinging.

"I love all these muscles, I could play with them for hours," she said, raking her nails down my stomach and my thighs.

"All I want to do is lick every single inch of your curves."

"Then do so," she teased before she swallowed the tip of my cock.

I groaned, head rolling back as I slid my fingers through her hair, changing the direction of her mouth so she could take me a bit deeper. She gagged slightly and I pulled back, but she gripped my hips, fingernails digging into my ass, and went harder, sucking me down and breathing through her nose.

She was so warm and wet it was hard for me to breathe, so I pulled out to keep myself from coming. She looked up at me with wide eyes and swollen lips, and she was the most beautiful thing I'd ever seen in my life.

We tumbled onto the bed, mouths clamped together, bodies pressed as one. She was soft and sweet, and I was hard and calloused, but it didn't matter. We didn't need to think of futures, or the fact that I liked her far more than I should.

That I wanted more than just this. But I couldn't have it, neither could she.

We were each other's distractions, nothing more, nothing less.

I kissed up and down her body, playing with her breasts, sucking her nipples until they firmed into hard points. She bit and sucked and licked down my body, playing with my cock, scraping her nails down my body.

I would have marks just like her, and it made me grin.

She got on all fours and I gripped her hips, plunging deep inside her, both of us calling out at the motion.

She pressed back into me when I would've waited, so I moved, hovering over her as I bit down on her shoulder, just enough to leave a mark, but not hard enough to hurt. She groaned, rocking her hips back with each thrust. I continued to play with her breasts as I pulled her up so her back was pressed against my chest. But we were leaning backwards so I went even deeper, and I could take her mouth with my own.

We were sweat-slick and barely able to catch our breaths but it didn't matter. This was everything that I had wanted, everything I knew I couldn't have. In the bliss of near orgasm I nearly shouted I needed her to stay. That I wanted her to stay.

But I wouldn't. Because that was just a pipe dream, the bliss of fucking. It wasn't anything real. It wasn't true.

She came again, my fingers on her clit, that swollen nub hard against my fingers, she whispered something I couldn't hear, or perhaps I didn't want to hear.

I followed her into that bliss, both of us collapsing in a heap of limbs and sweat and need and desire.

I was not going to fall in love with Lark Thornbird.

I could barely hold my own head up without hating the world around me.

I was the darkness that blocked Lark's brightness.

I didn't need to be her shadow. And she didn't need me at all.

Chapter Ten

East

I looked over Lark's notes, annoyed. It felt as if she were constantly on my mind, constantly there no matter what I did. It didn't help that my family seemed to be pushing her towards me. Even if they didn't know what the hell we were doing.

At least, I didn't think they knew. Trace might, because we hadn't been all that subtle. But my brothers and sisters-in-law would've brought up Lark by now if that was the case. Well, I had been avoiding them, but I wasn't going to think about that.

"Is this going to be a mineral pool or something?" one of the workers asked.

I nodded. "Yeah. I don't know what it's for beyond that. Detoxing? Making your skin feel nice? Or just to float so you feel better about yourself? I don't know."

The guy snorted. "Well, I guess if it makes you money."

I narrowed my gaze at him and shook my head. "We're not trying to swindle anybody," I said dryly.

The other man held up his hands quickly. "Oh, I didn't think you were. But you know. It's just not something I would do."

"Do I look like a guy who's going to go sit in water that other people have been sitting in? I don't even like pools."

"You know, I don't either. Anyway, got to get back to tile work."

I nodded, let the other guy go, and then glared down at my notes. There was still so much shit to do, and Eli and the others were working on hiring someone for the position. Once that person got here, I wouldn't have this on my plate. As it was, I had to work on baseboards in one of the older cabins we hadn't rehabbed yet, put in new flooring, and start painting the spare dining room that we had for larger groups.

That was all on my list, and I would get it done this week, but with this spa shit added to it, it felt like this was never-ending.

But at least Lark's notes were helpful. That was one burden off my shoulders at least. I needed to thank her because I wasn't good at shit like that. Maybe I'd ask her over for dinner or something. I figured I was decent at cooking since it was my role in the family before Kendall had come along. I was particular in what I made, but I figured that was just because I was an asshole, not because I was good at it. Though Kendall always said differently. And since she knew what she was doing, maybe I wasn't as mediocre at it as I thought.

Lark was either cooking for herself or eating with the girls. She didn't leave the property at all, mostly because once she did the world would know she was here, and she was enjoying her anonymity.

I paused. Asking her over for dinner would be past the whole friends or enemies or whatever the fuck we were with benefits. Wouldn't it? That would be like a date.

And I didn't date. I didn't date because as soon as I did, things got too real and they didn't like who I was. They walked away because they didn't want to deal with the hell that I had gone through. Didn't want to deal with the fact that sometimes I couldn't deal.

And Lark was going to leave, no matter what.

But before I could get more lost in those thoughts, a familiar voice echoed into the room.

"Hey, we need to talk."

I turned to see Eli standing there, Evan behind him. The crew all looked up and I waved them off. "Get back to work," I said. The contractor nodded and started directing everyone. I turned, gesturing for my brothers to leave the building.

"Come on, I'm not in the mood to do this here."

I didn't know what *this* was, but from the glares on their faces, I wasn't going to want to deal with it.

"Okay, what did I do now?"

All five of them stood there, arms crossed over their chests, glaring at me.

Great. Exactly what I needed.

"Why weren't you going to tell us you had a friend here?" Eli asked.

I stiffened because I hadn't realized it was going to be about Lawrence. I was ready to defend whatever the hell I was doing with Lark. I was ready to deny and get angry.

But Lawrence? Shit. I was going to kill Trace.

"Don't get mad at Trace," Everett said as he put up his hands, reading my mind. "We were going over the security briefing, or at least Eli was, and one thing led to another, and we had to go over the incident that we saw on the screen."

"Great, now I'm a note in some incident report?"

"I don't think you would be if you had talked to us. What the hell is going on, East?" Elijah asked, his voice low. "We know something happened. And you're the one who told me to get my head out of my ass when I was so far lost in my grief that I didn't see what was right in front of me. That I was pushing you guys away and hurting myself and you. So, let's talk it out."

"It's the middle of the workday. You're really going to do this now?" I asked, my palms going clammy. What the hell was wrong with me? It hadn't always been this bad. I was dealing. Finally, I was dealing. Yet it felt like it was all too much.

What the hell?

"Talk to us," Elliot said. "You know we've all been there. In one way or another, we all saw things that we don't want to think about. We all went through things that haunt us, and while it was harder for some of us, we've *all* been through it. And the reason that we're doing this now instead of later is that you keep avoiding us. You haven't come to dinner with us in over a week, you're not talking to us—the only person you're even talking to these days is Lark, and you always yell at her." Elliot was a little pointed with that, and I growled.

"Fine. Fine. I got out when I did because I didn't want to deal with the bureaucracy or the fighting or losing more friends. The timing of the attack was just pure coincidence," I explained.

"You never did tell us what happened over there," Everett whispered.

We stood in a clearing, far enough away from the rest of the guests that no one would overhear us. I closed my eyes, listened to the grackles, to the wind and the tall oaks, felt the sun beat on my face, and the cedar pollen in the air which made me want to scratch my eyes. This was home now, though it hadn't always been. We were still learning what that all meant.

But this was home.

"What happened?" Eli asked gently, and I sighed, finally ready to tell them.

When I returned to the US, getting out and ready to start whatever the next phase of my life would be, I'd only told them it was time. They had seen the signs, knew I was in mandated therapy because of the PTSD. Elliot and I had bunked together at first, and so Elliot had woken up to my nightmares, to my screams.

They had seen me patch up holes in the walls when I had punched too hard. They'd seen me get better, and now they were watching me fall apart again.

And while they had asked, they had never pushed.

But Lark knew now. So did Trace. And I was done hiding it.

I didn't know why I'd hidden it. Because, of all the people in my life, my brothers had never judged. Because they had seen their own hells and survived.

Why couldn't I?

"What about this Holmes guy?" Evan asked, scowling. "Why the hell would he blame you when he got out, too? In fact, from what you said he didn't even get hurt. You did."

I paused, trying to figure out how to answer, but it was Elliot who spoke instead, giving me a clearer understanding of his mind than I'd had in a long while.

"Sometimes it's those who come out unscathed who end up the worst. Who feel their scars more deeply when no one else sees them. He blames you, because it's easier than blaming himself. Even though neither of you deserve the blame. What occurred is unfair, it wasn't right, and it shouldn't have happened. But it's not your fault. And it wasn't Holmes's either. Is he still writing you?" Elliot asked.

I nodded. "About once a month. Usually in the middle of the month."

Eli cursed, the others joining in. "Why the hell didn't you tell us? Are you keeping those notes?"

I nodded tightly. "Yeah."

Elijah narrowed his gaze. "Not because you need them in case something happens, but because you feel like it's your penance. Am I wrong?" Elijah asked. Considering Elijah had blamed himself for his girlfriend's death, he understood.

"What of it?"

"Show them to Trace," Eli ordered.

"You might be my older brother, but you're not my boss." I growled.

"You are my brother. My co-owner, and you're going to fucking do what I say or all of us are going to gang up on you. Hell, I'll break into your house right now and get those letters myself and give them to Trace. He'll help us figure it out. He's here to keep our family safe. And that means keeping us safe from ourselves."

"What the hell do you want me to do?" I shouted. "There's nothing I can do. He hates me. What am I supposed to do about that? He hasn't hurt me. He just needs something or someone to be angry with. And maybe he doesn't have five asshole brothers that he can beat on."

"You wish you could beat on us," Evan snarled. "But we can take you down, little brother."

"Fuck off."

"No, I don't think so," Everett replied.

My twin glared at me, and it was like looking into a mirror, literally this time. Because Everett hated every moment of this too, but I didn't know how to fix this. I just wanted it to go away, but it wasn't going to. Not right then.

"What do you want me to do? I went to the funerals when I could. When I was home and healed, I met with the families of those we lost. And Holmes did too. And he hated that I survived and the others didn't. And when Lawrence got home, Holmes hated me even more. Because Lawrence was proof that we had left them behind. I don't know what the hell I'm supposed to do about it."

"Go talk with him," Eli said. "Talk with Lawrence. If he blames you, and hates you, then take it, and we'll deal with it with you. But it's tearing you up inside not to know, and honestly, it'll be good for you. If you want us to be with you, we will."

"I can handle it myself."

"Can you?" Elliot asked, his voice so soft I could barely hear it over the breeze.

"What am I supposed to do?" I asked.

"Ask for help. We're here for you. Just let us help."

"I'm not good at this. I've never been good at this."

"Maybe not, but you don't have to be. We're here to help you. Let us."

I turned away and looked out on the property that had been ours for a few years now.

There wasn't an event going on right now, because a major one was tomorrow. A wedding where Alexis, Eli's wife, was working her ass off making sure that it went off without a hitch, with Elliot pitching in where he could. Maddie was at the winery now most likely, going through a tour of the vineyard, doing a wine tasting, and enjoying cheese and whatever else Kendall brought over from the kitchens. Kendall had her restaurant and was doing the catering for the wedding, and was about to have a second restaurant that was even more elevated on the property in the next year or two. Bethany and Lark were somewhere on the property most likely, and with every passing month we added people to our team and into our family, and none of it seemed real. The cabins were scattered about the property, hidden within trees or clumped together. People milled about the square walkway where they were taking photos. There were others sitting around firepits that weren't lit yet, as it was still daylight, but they were enjoying themselves, drinking sparkling water or champagne. The large former barn turned wedding venue was empty, except for the people prepping it for the reception the next day.

The property spilled over acres and acres of Wilder land.

I didn't know how we had come to be here.

One instance I was ducking bullets, shouting at people to stay down as I went to find my fallen friends.

The next I was standing on land that I owned, land that I put my blood, sweat, and tears into, my brothers standing silently beside me, not pushing, and yet doing just that.

How was this my life? How was this our life?

They were all moving on, moving off property into homes that were better suited for families. I was an uncle, through my little sister and two of my brothers. The next wedding for the family was coming up in a matter of days, with bachelor and bachelorette parties and rehearsals underfoot.

We were growing, looking to the future, and all I could do was hold onto a past that didn't make any sense.

"What good will talking to Lawrence do?" I asked after a moment, my thoughts finally settling down. While we Wilders yelled at each other more often than not—as it was one of the best ways for us to get anything out of each other—we also let each other breathe, to come through our own thoughts. It was the only way we could focus. After all, we hadn't been a close family for years. We had been spread all over the world, barely talking because there hadn't been time. And now we were thrust together, living together, working together, and being up in each other's business.

"Even if it just helps him, it'll be worth it," Elliot said. "He has something to say, and you need to let him. Holmes has had his say enough, but Lawrence hasn't. And frankly, maybe you need to speak too."

I turned to him then, and I wanted to ask why it hurt so much, but he was just as closed off as I was. Maybe the others didn't see it because they weren't as close to the

137

edge as we were. Or maybe they saw enough to ensure that we wouldn't fall.

"Maybe. Maybe I should."

"Damn straight," Evan grumbled.

Eli cleared his throat as Everett moved forward. "And what about Lark?"

I froze, my heart beating fast. I tried to calm it down before my brothers could hear it.

"Huh?" I asked, not sounding as nonchalant as I wanted to.

"What's going on between the two of you?"

"She's just here. Nothing's going on."

"Don't fucking lie to us," Elijah snarled.

Elliot leaned back on his heels and just stared at me.

"What?" I asked.

"We all know you're sleeping with her," Eli answered.

"What's going on between you two?" Everett asked again.

"It's none of your business," I snarled. I should've known they would figure it out. We had been trying to be somewhat discreet, because as soon as my brothers knew, then the rest of the property would know, and then the rest of the world would know. I didn't need them up in our business. I didn't need the world and the media asking when Lark would write her next song about the person that was going to break her heart.

"She's our business, just like you are," Everett whispered.

"Fuck off," I snarled.

"Just don't hurt her," Elliot said. "And don't hurt yourself."

I stood there, the words slapping me, and I shook my head, not wanting to think.

Because this moment with Lark was just that, a moment.

It wasn't going to be something beyond sex.

It couldn't.

I wouldn't let it.

Chapter Eleven

Lark

"You stand in front of me, begging for another chance. Yet the one time I asked for more, you ran before you could leave me again."

"Not Mine" written by Lark Thornbird

I threw my hands in the air and belted out the next lyric, the mic in my hands and the music humming in my veins, as Bethany bumped me from the side, and we laughed.

"You thought you were everything and yet you were never the one. I promised myself that I would be on the run. And you're the one standing in front of me now, not kneeling, not groveling, doing nothing but shouting to the world. I was never yours and you were never mine. And you'll walk away, but I'll always be on your mind."

The rock music beneath the lyrics hummed, and we danced, shaking our heads and our asses at the same time, laughing at the bubbles of champagne in our system along with the lyrics.

This wasn't Bethany's bachelorette party, this was a party for just the two of us, as we sang karaoke on her back porch.

Everett stood in the doorway, laughing as he sipped his beer, and I knew that we were probably a little too much for him. But he was in love with Bethany, so he was going to have to deal with her best friend.

A few guests had walked by. They hadn't taken photos, but they had stopped, maybe to listen, maybe to be in awe of how ridiculous we were. So when one of them began clapping along, I hopped down from the porch and tilted the mic towards the other woman. She blinked at me with her wide eyes, before she sang along with the chorus, as if she wasn't just a stranger here for a night out with her significant other. The man at her side joined in, his bass adding the perfect blend to our voices.

Bethany clapped from the porch, dancing along with Everett as I sang with another guest, and then another.

By the end of the next song, we had a big crowd enjoying themselves, with only one person filming. Well, that was going to happen. They would put it on social media and then it would be another thing that people would talk about, but this was fun. And I was sharing music with strangers, something I did day in and day out. I didn't mind now. People would talk, because they always wanted to nitpick everything I did, and the same with Bethany.

But when the person put their phone in their pocket and grimaced, I shrugged and brought the mic to them. They sang along, their voice soft but sweet, and I kept moving, kept dancing along. The next song came on, and I handed the mic over to one of the guests and I leaned against the porch rail, grateful when Bethany handed me a sparkling water.

"By the way, that guest with the camera told Everett that they weren't going to post it. That it was just for them. Don't know if I believe them, but it's their right."

"We're on your home property. You can tell them not to."

Bethany shrugged. "I know. But this is our life now. The next house we live in will have different security, one that isn't on commercial property. So it'll be more private."

I nodded. "Yes, it's a little different here. A little twisty with the rules. But if they want to post that, it's just us having fun, nothing wrong with that."

"And it's not like you're dancing with a certain Wilder, so they can't get any wild ideas."

I froze and looked up at her. "You mean your future husband? Because that might bother people."

Bethany tapped her finger on my nose and just shook her head. "You're so cute. We all know that you and East have something. You okay?"

I pressed my lips together and looked towards the group of people that weren't our inner circle as they finished the last song and said their goodbyes, leaving the mic with Everett.

"Understood. But when we're in private, I will be asking many, many questions."

"I have no idea what you're talking about. I haven't done anything."

"It sounds like you're protesting a little too much."

"You know what it sounds like? Like I am going to head home and eat something for dinner."

"I didn't mean to push you away. I just want to know what's going on with you."

We were alone now, the crowd being gently herded off by security, even if I didn't think they noticed it was happening. Everett had gone to talk with Jason, so we had a moment of privacy.

"Nothing's going on with me. I'm just working. I can work anywhere."

"And you're heading to the studio soon?"

I nodded. "The time's set up for after the wedding. We've got to get another album out."

"Maybe we can build a studio on the Wilder property. You know, like the commune we are."

I laughed, shaking my head. "No, I don't think that needs to happen. Unless you want to build a whole set for YouTube. Do like a TV show on Wilder property."

Bethany shuddered. "Let's not give them any ideas. Not that I think that's something they would ever want to do. But now you're changing the subject. You're getting quite good at that."

"I learned from the best," I teased, fluttering my eyelashes.

"Seriously though. What is going on with you? You were up in the northeast, writing, and now you're down here. Is there something that you're fighting? Something I can help with?"

I nearly shook my head, but then I looked down at my open palms and sighed. "I was having a hard time with the album at first, because it felt like I had written about all the feelings I'd ever had. For some reason I felt like I would never have another one. Which is ridiculous and insane."

"You've never had issues like that before. Is it just stress?"

"I don't know. Maybe it's just life. I am not the young new thing on the airwaves these days. They're looking at the next teenage sensation."

"Yes, because you and AARP are one and the same."

I rolled my eyes. "I'm not even talking about that. But my voice is changing as I grow older. I'm not a teenager with a guitar anymore. I'm finding my own groove and my own genre. And I want to write what I want to write, but I also have to do the thousand other things that come with it. I know you understand that."

"I do," Bethany said with a pause. "And I understand that it's not easy when everybody has so many expectations of you."

I sighed and nodded. "So many expectations it's a little worrying. But you understand that, just like I do."

"I won an Oscar once, and that was one more time than I ever thought I would. So now I feel like I have to do it again, and my follow-up has to be even better. Or I'm a sellout if I go do something that's going to make me more money. Or I'm not doing enough indie flicks that won't give me any recognition or money, but will bring me prestige."

"So basically all of that, but with a Grammy. If I don't write something that is in a movie soundtrack that's nominated for an Oscar, then I'm not good enough. If I don't do a world tour that hits most major cities for fifty-two weeks,

I'm not enough. And I'm so grateful that these are the types of problems I even have, it's a privilege. But it's scary, because what if I'm not enough? What if I don't write what I want to and I sell out? What if selling out really isn't selling out, and it's writing what I want? I just need to sit down and do it, but I also want to take a break. It's just so confusing."

"And falling for East at the same time probably isn't helping."

I whirled at my best friend. "I'm not falling for East."

"You have the same look that I did when I fell for Everett. And don't forget, they're twins. It's a little ironic that my best friend is falling for my fiancé's twin brother."

I closed my eyes and groaned. "This sounds like a soap opera."

"No, it would only be a soap opera if they traded places. And if they ever did that, I would have to murder you all and it would be a whole thing. I'd rather not be on the news for that."

She laughed as she said it, and I joined in, shaking my head. "There's something seriously wrong with me."

"The only thing that's wrong with you is that you're not telling me what you feel."

"I don't know what I'm feeling. How am I supposed to figure that out?"

"You write about feelings every day."

"I write about them. But sometimes it feels like I don't *feel* them. I don't live through them. I don't know what I feel for East. And I don't want to talk about it because if I do, then it's real. And when I leave here? It's going to hurt if I let myself feel. So I'm not going to."

"Lark."

"I know. I know. I'm just setting myself up to fail."

"I'm not saying that. But maybe you should trust yourself enough to fall."

"Trust myself, or trust him?"

She had no answer for that, so we sat down, finished our waters, and when Everett came back to the porch, I said my goodbyes and made my way back to my cabin.

I nodded at Jason from where he kept guard, because that was his job, and I couldn't just have a normal day.

Someone stepped out onto the path and I nearly screamed before I realized who it was, and Jason murmured something to the other man before leaving. He stood under the path light, and tilted his head as he stared at me. "Did I scare you?"

"Only a lot." I said with a laugh. He shook his head and held out his hand. I wanted to reach out, to hold him close, to figure out exactly what that feeling was, but I held myself still.

"What is it?"

"I heard you sing. I was watching like a creeper from

the trees as I was finishing my work for the day," he clari-
fied, his eyes filled with laughter.

He looked so much lighter. I wanted to ask him about
his day and see what had happened. But it wasn't my
right. I knew that. But I wanted to know so much more.

When he frowned at me, I realized his hand was still
outstretched. I quickly took it, not wanting to make a
scene, but knowing that it was really because I just
wanted to touch him.

I was becoming addicted, and it was already a problem. But I wasn't going to stop. Not yet, maybe not ever.

"Why didn't you come and join in?"

East snorted. "I can sing sometimes. Mostly because I
have that baritone going for me."

"I always found that a little rude that most guys can
sing in that register, so no matter what their voice is
decent."

"You go soprano or alto, it's sexy."

"Look at you, knowing the words." I blushed in the
moonlight. "But thank you."

"I guess it was a compliment. It was mostly just the
truth." He shrugged as he said it, leading the way back to
my cabin. He was so surly, and I didn't know why it was
so attractive. On anyone else, I would hate it. There was
something seriously wrong with me.

"Come on, let's get inside."

"Oh, what are we going to do in there?" I asked, not buzzed at all from the champagne earlier, but still feeling bubbly.

He lowered his brows, smiled. "I don't know. Guess we'll figure it out."

I just shook my head and let him lead me inside.

"Got any cheese?" he asked out of the blue, and I blinked and nodded. "Oh, yes, I do."

"You want something to drink?"

"I can get it. I have some iced tea I made. Does that sound good?"

"Yeah, that sounds good. I had a beer earlier with the guys, and now tea sounds great."

Everything just felt off, a little weird, and yet...right? I wasn't sure, but instead of saying anything, I poured the tea as he opened up a can of tomato soup that Bethany had left, and heated it up as he slapped together a grilled cheese. "I've never been good at making grilled cheese," I said, and he raised a brow at me.

"Something you're not good at? I need to mark this down."

I rolled my eyes and flipped him off when he just grinned.

The grin looked good on him, and I was still so confused. Why was he here? Did I want him to be here? *Of course I did.*

149

"I never know how much butter to put on the bread, if it goes inside or outside, and then I end up making a hole in it or squishing the bread when I'm trying to turn it. Or the cheese doesn't melt. Or it burns. I can cook many things, never as good as Kendall, but I really can't do this."

He just stared at me and shook his head. "I'll teach you how to do it. Let me show you."

"Well, you haven't burned down the place yet, so that counts as something."

"I would hope so," he said with a laugh.

This felt like the most normal thing in the world, and yet, I was so afraid for everything to fall. But I pushed that out of my mind and let myself just be. Because when this bubble burst, I would have to deal. But not right now.

"So, how was your day?" I asked, trying to be casual about it. He looked at me then, gestured towards the pan as he flipped the grilled cheese like a professional. It looked perfectly brown, crisp and buttery, and my mouth watered.

"It was good. My brothers cornered me though,"

I froze and looked up at him. "Really?"

"Well, about a few things. One was you."

I cringed. "Bethany did the same thing."

He just shook his head. "Nosy. The lot of them. Of course, I'm pretty sure we were nosy about the others."

He placed both sandwiches on plates next to the

bowls of soup, and we stood there, eating next to one another, not bothering to sit. Everything felt like we had done this a hundred times, but I wasn't going to think about it too hard. I couldn't.

"What did they say?"

He shrugged and took a bite of his grilled cheese. I did the same and moaned at the taste. "This tastes so good."

"It's pretty simple. Not sure how you can fuck it up."

"Yet I will next time I try."

He shrugged, took another bite. "I'll try to teach you next time then, too."

Next time. Because there would be a next time. Or maybe he was just saying that.

"As for my brothers, they were just nosy."

There wasn't much that he could say there, but I nodded. "Bethany too. But we're girls, so I guess we talk a bit more."

"You haven't met my brothers. Pretty sure they could win the Olympics at talking about their feelings these days. I have no idea how the fuck that happened." He rolled his eyes, I just laughed.

"I would say I'm sorry, but it is kind of enlightened."

"You say enlightened, I say annoying as hell."

"Anyway, they also talked about Lawrence." He paused and finished off his sandwich before he went to finish the rest of his soup.

I was still chewing the first half of mine, so I kept eating, waiting for him to speak.

"I told them everything. And yeah, they pushed me to talk, but I did it."

"Are you okay?"

"I guess. Same as before. I think I'm going to talk with Lawrence though. Lawrence deserves that."

"Oh. That's good."

"Yeah. I guess so. What about you? How was your day?"

I nearly choked on my grilled cheese, but I swallowed and nodded. This all felt so normal. I didn't know why this was happening, but I wasn't going to stop it.

"I worked on a few things for the studio today; I know I'm going to have to go in and actually record soon. But I'm still writing."

"Yeah? What are you working on? An album, right? Or songs for someone else?"

"On my album. I'm thinking of making it a narrative album. Well, I'm past thinking right now and actually doing it."

"What does that mean?"

"It's going to be a story. I'm writing about a fictional person. The way the person is surviving. But they need to do more than that."

He tilted his head. "And that's not you?"

I smiled, knowing that I had told him my most personal parts of myself, and he never judged me, never made me feel worthless. And I honestly never thought he would, because he was East. That's not the kind of man he was. Though I wasn't sure he saw himself that way.

"This isn't about me. None of my songs are. Or perhaps all of them are. It's a weird thing. I guess you have to be a writer to understand it."

"Maybe. But you're smiling, so maybe it's working."

He finished off his soup, then gestured towards mine so I would finish eating. We talked about the rest of our days, and something worrying slid into me. Because no. Oh no. I could not fall for this man.

I couldn't love him.

Even though I was pretty sure I was already well on my way.

Chapter Twelve

East

The next morning when my alarm went off, I rolled to the side, reaching from my phone, only to realize it wasn't there. Eyes still closed, I patted around on the night table, hitting a lamp that I didn't recognize, and then a paperback book that wasn't mine.

I squinted, looked around, and realized that I wasn't in my room. No, I was in Lark's cabin.

Hell. I had stayed the night? I hadn't meant to stay the night. That wasn't something that we did.

"Your phone's over here," Lark whispered, her voice still soft, with the slight rasp of sleep. It was that voice that had called to me first. Through her songs, through the way that she could enrapture you with just a single note.

"Do you want me to turn off your alarm?" Lark asked

as she picked up the phone, unplugged it from its charger, and handed it over.

"I've got it, thanks," I said, pressing the end button before sitting up and running my hands through my hair. "I'm glad that alarm is automatic during the week, or I would've slept in."

Lark sat up and stretched, her bare breasts catching my attention. She didn't bother to cover herself up, instead she rolled her shoulders and neck, before rubbing her lower back.

"I'm glad you did too. I guess we fell asleep early last night." She paused, and then reached for the sheets, covering herself up. I hated losing the view, but then reminded myself I had things to do for the day, and I shouldn't be here. She was going to leave soon. To head back to her everyday life, a life that had nothing to do with me.

It would behoove me to remember that.

"I have to head out. I've a few meetings, and then I have to work on my never-ending to-do list."

She smiled tentatively at me. What did she want me to say? Did she *want* me to stay?

I hadn't been in this position before. I'd been with women, sure. But never for more than a few nights, and I never slept over.

Now, it was different, and I didn't know what I was supposed to do—what I should do about it.

"What are you doing today?" I asked, feeling awkward as hell.

She smiled then, that sweet smile that said she was thinking of something she wouldn't tell me. I wanted to know. I needed to stop though, because she wasn't going to stay.

"I have a few meetings too, and work. And then I am heading to the bachelorette party." She grinned.

I winced. "Hell. I forgot that was tonight."

"Is the bachelor party tonight too?" she asked, her eyes dancing with laughter.

That did something to me, but I ignored it. It was better not to think about that.

"Yeah. Though I think we're just hanging out at the winery. Everett didn't want much, and we're not going to force him into strip clubs or something."

Lark rolled her eyes. "Oh yes, because I could totally see the Wilder brothers at a strip club."

"Hey, we used to party back in our day."

"You say that as if you're all over the hill."

"Sometimes it feels like it," I said, before I stretched my shoulders a bit. "I need to go."

There was something else in those words, something I knew that neither one of us were going to think about. She nodded, her eyes going a little sad before she blinked it away.

"Of course. I'll be here for a little bit. Anyway, last night was nice."

I didn't think she meant the sex. No, she meant something else. Something neither one of us was going to admit, and I was grateful for that.

I nodded and leaned down, pressing my lips to hers quickly. "Have a good day. I guess I need to go fix things."

She looked at me then. "Do you mean with your job? Or with Lawrence."

I stiffened, but nodded. "Yeah. I need to talk with him in a bit. I don't know how much longer he's going to be on the property."

"You've got this, East."

She did that little half-smile thing, one that reached her eyes and yet made her look sad at the same time. I wanted to believe her. But I wasn't even sure I believed myself. I picked up my things and headed out.

I made it to my cabin and quickly showered, before getting ready for the rest of the day. I had a shit ton to do, and I wasn't in the mood to do any of it, even though I didn't have a choice.

I replied to a few texts from my brothers, most of them confirming that we were meeting at the winery for the bachelor party, and figured that a little bit of wine, a shit ton of food, and us just talking about nothing was a damn good bachelor party for us.

I knew that the girls were going to one of the smaller venues on our property, one where they would have some privacy with some of Bethany's friends from LA, as well as the girls from here. Hopefully Trace and the others would be able to keep it secure, even though Trace was going to hang out with us tonight too. Double duty, friend and bodyguard.

Speaking of double duty, I headed out the back door of my cabin and into the maintenance cabin next door. This was where I kept everything I needed to keep the Wilder Retreat and Winery running. I had a team for the winery equipment because that wasn't my expertise, though I was learning and was better than I had been. I also did the plumbing and electrical and a lot of the contracting for this place. I learned everything that I possibly could in order to actually help, and not feel like I was just tacked onto this family project because I didn't have any other skills.

I frowned, wondering why that came to mind again.

I knew my worth. Or at least I had.

I picked up my tool belt and a few other things, and got to work. Naomi needed me to work on something behind the desk. All of the wood grain trim and other attachments were original to the building, so if something was broken, it needed to be fixed correctly, and not just taped together.

As I made my way to the building, I saw a familiar face and swallowed hard. I set my toolbox on the bench beside me.

Lawrence spoke with a blonde woman, the two of them laughing underneath the morning sun, coffee in their hands. There were four kids, between twelve and eighteen I thought, if I remembered their ages right, laughing with one another, as they played with the life-size chessboard on the property.

They were a family, a big family.

It seemed crazy to me that he was able to have all of that.

Lawrence's wife saw me first, her eyes widening for a bit before she smiled. She reached out and gently put her hand on Lawrence's arm, leaned forward, whispering something to him.

He turned, his eyes widening fractionally, before he gave me a tentative smile.

That was on me. That hesitant smile. That worry. He had nothing to worry about. This wasn't on him. This was me.

I needed to be better than this.

I cleared my throat, raised my hand in an awkward wave. Lawrence tilted his chin and gestured for me to come over. I let out a breath and thought of what Lark told me, and what my brothers had said.

Lawrence deserved to speak to me. And I deserved not to hide. Lawrence had come back, our friends hadn't, but he had. And so had I. I needed to be better than this.

Bile rose in my throat, that familiar feeling of an episode coming on, so I held my breath for a count of five, before I released it and put one foot in front of the other.

"Hey, East. Good morning," Lawrence said cautiously, lifting his coffee up in a gesture of hello.

I nodded at him and his wife.

"Good morning. You guys having fun?" I asked, my voice a little gruff.

Lawrence cleared his throat before smiling at me, this time a little bit brighter than before. I wasn't yelling, wasn't running away. This was already off to a better start.

"We're heading out this afternoon, but the kids wanted to play with this chess set."

I smiled as I gestured towards it. "It was half broken when we bought the place, but we found a woodworker to help us with the pieces, and I painted them myself. That's probably why one of them is starting to chip," I said, a little self-deprecatingly.

Lawrence laughed, shaking his head as his wife joined in.

"East, let me introduce you to my wife. This is Victoria, and our kids." He gestured for the kids to come over. "Come and meet my friend. This is Gabby, Jeremy, Nick, and Kristie. All in age order," he said, as Gabby rolled her eyes.

"Thanks, Dad."

"I'm still taller," Jeremy said, and I laughed.

"It's nice to meet all of you." And it was the truth. Lawrence looked happy. And that was damn good. Especially after everything that happened.

"Why don't I take the kids in to go get a table for breakfast, and you guys can talk."

"It was nice to meet you," the youngest, Kristie said. "Dad talks about you all the time." She smiled as she said it. Gabby rolled her eyes and tugged at her ponytail.

They grumbled at one another, the boys joining in, reminding me of me and my brothers and sister.

That made me smile, a little of the tension easing as Victoria kissed her husband's cheek and waved at me, before pulling the four teenagers away.

"Your kids are all grown up."

"Right? When did they get so big?"

"That's just crazy to me."

"I know, right? I still can't believe this is my life. I'm damn happy about it. But yeah. It's a little crazy to me, too."

"Are they good though? Do they know?" I asked, my voice low.

Lawrence met my gaze and nodded tightly. "They knew something happened, they remember me being gone, but they don't know everything. Only Victoria and my therapist know all of that," Lawrence said.

"I'm glad you can talk to her."

"Me too. She's everything to me. She held it together when I was overseas, and when I didn't come back on time. She's stronger than I'll ever be."

I thought about Eliza, my sister who had been the one waiting at home, who had gotten the flag when her first husband had died.

"Yeah. They're always the stronger ones. They have to hold everything together while we're gone, and then we come home, with no idea what the fuck is going on in our lives, and they have to try to piece us back together."

"Yeah, I figured you'd understand that. She raised our kids for the early years of their lives. I barely had anything to do with it. I wasn't in the country for it. And then I uprooted their lives more often than not. As soon as we were able to settle down, I'd have to move again. So when I came back that final time, I was done. We were all done. And now I get to be a dad. To figure out what the fuck I'm doing when it comes to raising these kids. Thankfully Victoria's a gentle teacher. Though she never should have had to, we should have been learning together."

"I'd say she knew what she signed up for. But that's just bullshit. You never know what you sign up for. And you're the one that did it."

"Damn straight. I'm just lucky that she loves me enough to stay."

There was an awkward silence, and I sighed before saying what I needed to. "I'm sorry. For leaving. For not getting you out in time."

Lawrence met my gaze, then set down his coffee mug on the pillar beside us. "It's not your fault. It never was. You were hurt, East. Do you not remember the concussion? The shrapnel in your hip and to your leg? You were bleeding all over the place. You and our guys. Only one of us didn't get hurt that day, and that was because he was on the other side. He was able to get you guys help."

"But I didn't get you help."

"It wasn't your fault. I got out. Finally. And I'm not always okay but I figure it out. Because I have to. I have a good support system. I know you went to the funerals—the ones that I couldn't go to because I wasn't out yet. And I know you came to the house."

I paused and stared at him. "What?"

"Victoria's mom finally told us how you went to pay your respects to Victoria and the kids, and her mom blocked you. I remember that. I remember her telling me that, and it took a while for it to click. Victoria's mom never understood why her daughter would marry an airman. Why she wanted to shackle herself to a system she didn't like. And I got that. Not everybody wants to be that way. Not everybody can do that and I don't blame them. I do blame the woman for pushing you away before Victoria had a chance to talk to you. And if you let her later, she'd want to apologize too for her mother's actions."

I froze, the memories of that day coming back. I had walked the long distance from where the cab had dropped me off to his house, and an older woman had blocked my access, hadn't let me go in to say I was sorry. To see if there was anything I could do. She had screamed at me and lashed out and pushed me away.

I had forgotten most of it. Because I hadn't been able to handle it.

"I didn't blame her for hating me. Though for some reason part of it twisted up in my head that it was Victoria not her mom."

"No, Victoria never blamed you. And neither did I."

"Well, Victoria's mom isn't the only one that blames me."

Lawrence cursed under his breath. "Oh. I know. He came to me, you know. After."

I froze. "What?" I asked, trying to keep up with what was going on.

"I never blamed you for anything. You got out, and you're building this life for yourself. I got home, and I'm trying to rebuild the life that I almost lost. But you and I? We're the same. We're making our way through. But Holmes? He hates me. He blames me for coming home just as much as you."

"You were captured. What the hell were you supposed to do?"

"And you got hurt. Practically bleeding out, as far as I can recall. Holmes was the only one who wasn't hurt, but in the end that wasn't really the case, was it? Not when he's lashing out like his foot is in a trap. So I don't fucking know. But he came to me, and blames me for their deaths. I don't know what I'm supposed to do about that, but I just wanted to let you know that *I* don't blame you. I blame the situation, and I blame the people that hurt me. But I don't blame you."

"Fuck Holmes. Just, fuck him."

"Does he write to you too?" Lawrence asked, and my head snapped up.

"Yes." I paused. "He writes to you?"

"Yeah. There's something wrong with him, East. And I don't know what the hell we're supposed to do about it. Just, be careful. He worries me. I'm glad that I am here to protect my kids. Because while we came back, I don't think all of Holmes did."

"I'm just glad that you're back," I said, not knowing what else to say.

"Hell, I'm glad you're back too. And that you are actually fucking talking to me."

"Yeah. That's pretty good."

Lawrence hugged me tight, and I squeezed him back like my life depended on it.

"Come on, do you have a minute before you have to work? You can come eat breakfast with us."

"My sister-in-law's the one cooking, so you'll have a damn good meal."

"Then join us. I know you have a thousand things to do but it would mean a lot to me. And then maybe later, we can plan some time to get together. And you can introduce me to your girl."

I shook my head. "She's not my girl."

"I know who she is by the way. I recognized her. Kind of wish she was your girl."

"Yeah. Right? I wish she was, too."

I wanted to call Lark, to tell her to join us, to tell her what happened. But I stopped myself.

She wasn't mine. She wasn't going to stay. I had already lost enough people. I didn't need to lose her too.

Chapter Thirteen

Lark

"The only part holding me back is you. But I know that's a lie from the moment I look in the mirror. Because I'm the one that makes that choice. And I can't choose you."

"Mirror" written by Lark Thornbird

"You know, even when I was twenty, I don't think I could move my hips like that," Kendall said to me as she leaned against my shoulder, drink in hand.

I laughed, watching Bethany and Maddie dance with a few of our friends from LA.

They looked like they were having the time of their lives, and they were. So were we. We were in a private room, dancing and laughing, eating amazing food—some Kendall had made, some we had brought in so she wouldn't have to work the whole day. We were enjoying ourselves out from under the watchful eye of the ever-present paparazzi.

Rumors had abounded that the wedding would be happening soon, even though we were keeping it private. However, Bethany and Everett had been strategic in sending rumors towards other parts of the world. Right now, the world thought that Bethany and Everett were heading to the Caribbean for a secret wedding. They were camped out in front of their LA home, with body doubles pretending to be the couple.

I shook my head at the thought, wondering how this was our life. It didn't make any sense to me, but thankfully, with the paparazzi and social media focused so much on Bethany and Everett's whereabouts in LA, they assumed I was there with them. Because of course I would be there for the wedding. So we were in hiding on Wilder land, no cell phones allowed other than for personal use.

Nobody knew where we were, and we were just enjoying ourselves.

The fact that two Oscar winners, a Tony winner, an Emmy winner, and a lead showrunner were all dancing around Bethany just made me laugh. We weren't going to be able to keep this secret for long, but long enough to hopefully get through tomorrow's wedding.

"Bethany's just drinking water now, right?" Alexis asked, coming forward with her tablet in her hand.

Kendall leaned down, plucked the tablet from her, and shook her head.

"She's got water, we are on our second glass of champagne, and you are going to go dance and have fun. You're not working right now, Miss Wedding Planner."

Alexis narrowed her gaze. "Damn straight, I'm working. I'm the one planning the wedding for tomorrow."

"And you're doing an amazing job," I said as I wrapped my arm around Alexis's shoulders. "But you're allowed to have fun too."

Alexis smiled, her eyes radiating joy even on top of the stress that came from the wedding.

"I am excited. I am going to have fun. More fun than I already am. However, I know my responsibilities. And that means working my ass off right now so we can enjoy ourselves tomorrow."

"Everything's going to be great. You don't need to stress out," Bethany said as she wrapped her arms around Alexis from behind.

Bethany was radiating joy, and she looked so damn happy, it made me just grin.

"I'm just so excited that you all are here. And I am finally marrying the love of my life. We've been together for over two years, and we're finally making it happen."

"He sure took his time," Alexis said as she took the glass of champagne from Maddie's hands. "The Wilder brothers are usually pretty quick off the mark when it comes to getting a ring on their girls' fingers."

Maddie laughed. "Yes, I'm pretty sure that Eli had you down the aisle before you guys even finished saying you were going to get married."

"I'm a wedding planner, he has a venue, it sort of just made sense."

"Evan and I were so quick to get married that we did it twice," Kendall said with laughter in her eyes.

It was good that she was smiling and laughing about the fact that she and Evan had divorced once but had come back together.

I loved the idea that love could conquer, maybe not all, but enough. And it took communication and painstakingly difficult conversations to make it happen.

"So wait, who here is getting married next?" Stacey, one of our friends from LA, asked.

"That would be me," Maddie said, sharing her beautiful engagement ring.

Everybody did the proper oohs and ahs as they looked at the diamonds surrounded by black stones, and Maddie beamed.

"I am very, very spoiled. But I'm okay with it because we work our butts off."

"You guys are just so great together. I'm glad that the next wedding's yours. I hope I get an invite," I teased.

"Of course you're getting an invite. But I will not ask you to be our wedding singer. Don't worry about that."

I finished off my champagne, then reached for my water. "I think I could make an exception for that. After all, I am singing at your wedding," I teased as I looked at Bethany.

"And I'm so blessed for that. Seriously though, I can't wait to start planning your wedding. I know we have to get through mine first, but yes, Wilder weddings are the best."

"And it's because I do plan a great wedding," Alexis teased as everyone laughed.

One of Bethany's friends looked at me. "What about you, Lark? Have you snatched any of the Wilder brothers? I hear there's two left. And some cousins?"

"The cousins will be here for the wedding," Kendall teased. "They arrive early tomorrow morning right before the wedding starts."

"I get to meet them. Finally," Maddie said as she clapped her hands.

"I'm pretty sure Lark has her eyes on a certain Wilder in particular," Kendall teased.

I glared at her and shook my head.

"It's not what you think."

"What's not what we think?" Stacey asked as the other girls from LA leaned forward, eager.

They would never gossip, whatever was said here would not leave this room, and yet I didn't want to make it a thing.

"I had my eyes on Evan. But then he went and got married to his ex-wife and it just ruined everything. All of my dreams. All of my happiness. All gone. But it's fine, I now swoon over all of the Wilder brothers. They're growly and bearded and beautiful. It's a little annoying," I teased as the girls laughed, though they looked a little disappointed that I wasn't sharing the details.

As the girls went back to dancing, Kendall sighed. "I meant to put you on the spot and didn't mean to put you on the spot at the same time."

"No worries. No spot taken."

"A lot of spots taken, whatever that means," Kendall said with a roll of her eyes. "So, it's not serious between you two?"

I looked down at my water and shrugged. "It's not. We're just having fun. Relieving stress and tension before we go back to the real world."

"I guess that's okay. Sex is great. And you should have whatever type of relationship you want. But is that the type of relationship you want?" she asked cautiously.

I didn't know what I wanted. But it wasn't like I was

going to say that. This wasn't the time or place for that conversation.

"We're just having fun. We have separate lives, and I know that. I knew what I was getting into when we started. For fun. That's it."

"When do you go back?"

I looked down at my hands and sighed. "In two days." I hadn't told East that yet, and I wasn't sure I could. "I have studio time booked, and I think I'm ready with this album. At least to start. I'm ready to get back to work, to get out there."

"Were you not ready before?"

"No. That kind of worries me. Music and writing have always been so easy for me. And yet I couldn't for a while."

"What changed?"

I sighed, but I didn't let myself answer truthfully. Not even to myself. "I took a break. I came here and I grounded myself. And now I will go home and work because I am blessed to have a job that I love. And I want to make sure that those who work for me and with me have jobs, and we will all do what we have to because I am reliable."

"And East isn't part of that," Kendall said, and there wasn't any animosity in that. Instead it was just sadness. Or maybe I was thinking too hard about her words.

"I knew what I was getting into," I repeated. "And we're having fun. And when we have to walk away, because that's what our lives demand, we'll remain friends. I'm not going anywhere for long—I love you guys, I love my family, and Bethany is part of that family. So you're not getting rid of me. But I'm not going to end up with East and become a Wilder and be all sparkly and fancy and everything that you seem to be wanting. That's not in the cards for me and that's fine. I'm okay."

I knew I sounded as if I was trying to reassure myself, and maybe I was. But in the end it didn't matter. I had what I had, and I didn't need anything else.

When the party ended, I walked back to my cabin at a leisurely pace, laughing along with the security team. There were no cameras, no fans wanting pictures or autographs. This was just private time, time that was slowly coming to a close.

I waved to Jason, then headed into my little cabin, and figured I would make myself a cup of coffee, and maybe get to writing.

That would be enough.

It would have to be.

When the soft knock came, I wasn't surprised. We hadn't made plans, but we knew our time would be coming to an end soon.

I opened the door and let him in, and before I could

say anything, he kissed me, a gentle kiss as he brushed my hair from my face. I sighed into him, lying to myself that this was okay.

"How was the party?" he murmured.

"Amazing. Relaxing. Fun. Bethany and Everett are going to have the best wedding ever."

"Damn straight. That's what we Wilders do."

Only not for him. He didn't want that, at least not with me. I reminded myself of that as he slowly walked me towards the bedroom.

This was becoming routine. A routine that would have to end soon. We stripped each other, talking about his time with his brothers at the bachelor party.

He tasted of wine, but his eyes were clear. He was here. With me.

He laid me down on the bed and covered me with his body. I let him, and opened myself for him.

"Too much champagne?" he asked, nibbling on my chin.

"No, why do you ask?" I teased, slowly trailing my fingers down his bare back.

"I don't know, you seem distant."

"No, I'm just thinking about tomorrow. But I don't want to right now. So kiss me."

He met my gaze, and I wanted him to say something. I wanted him to ask me to stay, to want something more.

He wasn't going to.

Neither of us was going to. I knew the rules when we started this. When we started to trust one another, and that meant we couldn't ask for more.

I slid my hands down his back, holding him close, and I just breathed him in. His fingers slid between my wet folds, bringing me closer to the edge, and when he slid deep inside me, his cock stretching me, I moaned for him.

"You're so beautiful," he whispered, and I hummed along him, arching my back so he could go deeper.

He sat up on his knees and gripped my hips, pounding into me. I gripped the headboard, keeping myself steady as my breasts bounced and my body shook.

He flipped us over so he was on his back and I was riding him, his hands on my breasts, keeping me steady as I rocked my hips, rolling over him. With this angle he was so much deeper, and I neared the edge.

When I finally came, I kept my eyes shut, knowing I couldn't look at him.

I didn't know what I wanted to see. Him wanting more. Or him having enough.

He came not long after, filling me, and pulled me close. I sucked in deep breaths, hoping that it looked like I was just trying to catch my breath, not that I was trying to keep back tears.

Because I was falling in love with him.

Only the problem was, I knew this love was a lie.

And he was going to break me.

Or rather, I was going to break myself.

I was going to become the lyrics I had never written, the lyrics I would never write.

I was my own song of pain and sorrow.

I was the author of my own heartache.

And I had only myself to blame.

Chapter Fourteen

East

People milled about, laughing with one another as they waited to be seated, and I adjusted my tie for the fifteenth time.

When Elliot slapped my hand again, I turned to him. "What?" I snapped, and my brother just raised a brow.

"If you fuck with your tie one more time, I'm going to take it off and throw it somewhere."

"And then you can deal with Everett when he realizes that I'm not wearing a tie."

"You know, the fact that they only wanted one person each up there, to keep the wedding from being too big, was kind of nice."

I shrugged and barely resisted the urge to fuck with my tie again. Elliot raised a brow at me so I figured he thought I was about to do it anyway.

"Well, with just our side of the family it's a little ridiculous."

The wedding would start in another twenty minutes or so, and people were still getting situated. My brothers were running around doing a hundred things at once, so it was odd that Elliot even had a moment to spare to talk with me. He had been working alongside Alexis and Trace for most of the morning. Nobody had caught wind that the wedding was happening today. *Thank God*, I thought.

There were no helicopters or paparazzi yet, but there were more than a few celebrities on the property. Everybody was doing their best to keep this under wraps, but we knew it couldn't last forever. We had to hope, but you just never knew.

Because I was Everett's twin, I had been the one elected to stand up for him. Any one of us would've done it, including Eliza. But he chose me. I wasn't going to screw this up.

Yet the tension in my stomach told me that if I wasn't careful, I just might. Because the person standing up with Bethany was of course the one person that I wanted, and the one person that I shouldn't.

"You know what you're going to do about Lark yet?" Elliot asked, his voice low so no one could overhear.

I froze, wondering when my brother got so good at reading my mind. "Don't know what you mean by that."

"You're really good at lying to yourself, but you've been shit at lying to us. What are you going to do?"

I looked at him and noticed the tiredness in his eyes, the fact that his hair was a little messed up—something that wasn't usual for him. Something was going on with my little brother, something he wasn't talking to me about. But I had been so lost in my own turmoil and whatever the hell was going on with Lark, that I hadn't realized before now.

I wanted to find out what was going on, to help him, but now wasn't the time.

"I'm fine. I don't know what's happening, I don't know if anything should happen. But it just is."

"That's not really an answer."

I sighed, shrugged. "I don't really have an answer to give you. Which sucks, I know. But I don't. She's leaving, Elliot. We're just having fun. I'm her distraction, and I'm okay with that."

"Again, with the lies. When did you get so good at them?" Elliot asked, his voice low.

"You just told me I wasn't."

"I did, didn't I?" Elliot studied my face for a moment before he cleared his throat. "I should head over. They want us in the front of the ceremony. Need to make sure I don't lose my spot."

"Like Alexis would let anyone take it."

"You never know." He let out a breath. "She makes you happy, you know. I don't know if you see it. But she does."

"Go sit down. It's really not like that."

"Yeah, then why is she looking at you right now?" He smiled as he walked off, and I turned to see Lark standing on the other side of the aisle, smiling at me.

I licked my lips, swallowing hard. Lark Thornbird was the most beautiful woman I had ever seen in my life. And I thought that long before I'd even met her. Her voice soothed souls, her smile radiated everything that a man could want. And I had always wanted her. And now that I'd had her, it felt like I was living in a dream that didn't make any sense.

"Wow."

She smiled then, and though we stood behind silk and lace curtains from the rest of the wedding guests, I still tried to be careful. I didn't need to make a scene, didn't need the world to see me look at her.

Because damn it, I looked.

She had on a dove-gray dress, one that brought out the color of her eyes. It molded around her breasts and tightened in at her waist before flaring down around her knees.

Was it a mermaid shape? I sucked at knowing dress types, but all I knew was that it fit her perfectly, and I really wanted to rip it off her.

The night before we'd slept together more than once, barely getting any sleep at all, now that I thought about it.

I hadn't even asked her if I was going to see her the night before, or if I would see her tonight. We had both just assumed, or at least I had, and she hadn't pushed me away.

But she was going to leave. And I was going to be left behind.

"You look amazing. Are you ready for this?" she asked, bouncing in her heels. She held a bouquet at her side, and her hair was half-up, and curled down her back. She'd done her eyes in a soft smoky style—I didn't know what it was called, I just knew she was beautiful.

"We don't have to do much, do we?"

"You still have to walk me down that aisle."

I cringed. "I guess I should have shown up to the rehearsal?"

There had been a water leak in one of the cabins during the rehearsal, and I'd had to go. Elliot had stepped in for me, and I felt like shit for not going to the rehearsal. I'd made it for the food, but that was it. Old buildings required a lot of work, and I worked my ass off on them, but that meant I missed out on some things.

"It's okay, I'll lead you through. Plus, you know, Alexis has notes."

I laughed, thinking of my sister-in-law. "Yeah, Alexis would have notes."

"Did somebody say my name?" Alexis asked as she came forward, her dress a different shade of gray.

"You look beautiful," I said to my sister-in-law as I leaned down and kissed her cheek.

"Oh, thank you for that. I'm just glad that I was able to leave the baby with the babysitter for now because I have a thousand things to do, and a crying toddler and set of twins isn't really helpful," she said, including Evan and Kendall's kids.

"Don't worry, they're coming to the party afterwards, right?"

"Yes. They'll be there. They're not quite old enough to hang out for the ceremony. Now, all you need to do is walk Lark slowly down the aisle, take your position by your brother, give him the rings when asked, and then after they are pronounced husband and wife, you take Lark back down the aisle after them. That's it. I really wish you would've practiced."

"I was in the other weddings. I've got this. I watch them for a living, you know."

Alexis just shook her head. "Next time, we're sending

Elliot to deal with the plumbing and you are doing the rehearsal."

"Sure. Because he's really going to let you do that."

"I can have hopes and dreams. Now, we have two minutes, Bethany's on her way. Everett is at his place already near Eli, who is officiating, and we're ready to go."

I smiled. "Go sit down. We've got this," I said.

"If you had actually been at the rehearsal, you know I'm not going to be sitting down this whole time. I'm not in the wedding, I'm doing a thousand things. Go, go, go."

And then, Bethany was behind us, and the silk curtains were moving, and I had my arm around Lark's.

She was so warm, so small. I did what Alexis said, and stepped slowly, this time following Lark's lead. She knew what she was doing. I was just following along. Which seemed like a symbol for something, but I ignored that thought. I just needed to get there.

When we stood at the end of the aisle, I froze for a moment, forgetting what I needed to do, yet all I could do was look down at Lark. She just grinned up at me, confusion in her gaze, before she leaned back and squeezed my hand.

"You've got this, go to your mark," she mouthed, and I nearly leaned down, captured her lips in my own.

That would have been inappropriate. What the hell was wrong with me?

Confused and wondering why I wanted to do that here, of all places, I went to my spot, and started to apologize to Everett, but he didn't have eyes for me.

No, they were all for Bethany.

She stood at the other end of the aisle, radiant in her soft wedding dress. She hadn't wanted traditional white, but wore a creamy white of some sort. I'm sure Alexis would know the color. Bethany looked gorgeous, as if she had been waiting for this moment for a lifetime. Then again, she had. Everett had, too.

A violinist began with some song I didn't recognize, and I watched as the love of my brother's life made her way down the aisle, her eyes only for Everett.

Eli cleared his throat and began.

When we first opened the Wilder Retreat, we hadn't known this was where we would be. Somehow though, we'd found our way. Eli had become an officiant so he could step in at the last minute if something arose, and for moments like this.

Our sister and her family sat in the chairs on the lawn underneath the eaves of the carved-out barn on the property. The rest of my brothers sat there as well, their families with them. The babies of course were with the babysitter. We were all there, waiting. Watching. Our cousins had come, and though we were many, Bethany's friends and workmates outnumbered us. Yet this was still private, still a small wedding.

And as the couple were married and kissed in front of us, as everyone cheered, I did my best to pull my gaze from Lark.

Because I saw the romance in her eyes, saw the tears.

And there was something damn wrong with me.

As Everett and Bethany laughed down the aisle, Everett twirling his bride, I held out my hand for Lark, who just shook her head.

"Please don't twirl me," she called out, laughing away her tears.

"I don't know, I could try."

Instead, I picked her up and carried her down the aisle, just to make her laugh, and ignored the curious glances.

We were just following along, and when Eli did the same for Alexis, Evan for Kendall, and Elijah for Maddie, I ignored the looks. Eliza of course jumped on Elliot's back, just to make him laugh, and he carried our youngest sister down the aisle, as the rest of the family and friends joined in, laughing, into this new phase of their lives.

I set Lark down and smiled at her.

"Well. That was interesting."

"You don't like weddings?" she asked, and I reached into my pocket for the handkerchief Alexis had given me.

"Yeah, but do you? You're crying."

"I'm crying because I'm happy," she teased, as I reached out and wiped another tear from her cheek.

"Really?"

"Yes, really. I'd say it's a girl thing, but that's sexist. Some people just cry at weddings. Get over it, Wilder."

"I see weddings every week. There are a lot of criers. I just assume it's because they're signing their life away."

I was teasing, and I hoped she knew that. She rolled her eyes and I was glad she got the joke. Because my brothers were happy. I knew happiness existed. Just not for me.

"I need to go help Bethany with a few things, but I'll see you soon." She practically ran off, and I had to wonder if I had done something. Maybe I had. Hell.

I went to go help my brothers make sure the setup for the reception was ready, and thankfully it was, because Alexis knew what the hell she was doing. And when they introduced the bride and groom to the dance floor, and the first dance went off without a hitch, my gaze kept traveling to Lark. She laughed with some of Bethany's friends, and she and Elliot danced around afterwards, as if they didn't have a care in the world.

I wasn't going to be jealous, but damn it, I was fucking jealous.

That's when I found myself in front of her, because I was an asshole.

"Dance with me?" I asked.

She looked at me then, blinking. "If-if you want to," she stuttered, and then her hand was in mine, and we were on the dance floor with the others.

She was so close to me, the music slow and soft, and it was all I could do not to kiss her right there.

But she was leaving.

She wasn't mine. I had been such a jerk to her for so long, I had been so cruel over little things; we both knew where we stood. I had been the one to put the barriers there with her.

I could feel her heartbeat, feel her soft breaths against my skin, and when I wanted to reach out, to touch my finger to her jaw, I refused. I saw the looks of those from LA who were wondering who the hell this guy was.

I needed to stop this. I couldn't have her.

"East?" she asked, her voice low. "What's going on in that mind of yours?"

The song ended, and I didn't realize we had stopped dancing, the others were moving around us. There was a faster song going now and the kids were out, laughing and dancing, and people were eating from the buffet, and it was as if the whole party was going on around us, and I was just trying to keep up.

"I'm sorry," I said, and I was. I couldn't handle this. My hands were going numb, and my throat hurt. My head pounded, and I knew what was coming. Another episode. I would be fine. I had handled this before. Sometimes with too much noise and too much everything, it felt like it was all going to explode. Just like everything had before. I left her standing there, staring at me, and I pushed past the others, ignoring shouts of my name. I just kept going.

The ground beneath me rumbled, and I took a few steps, trying to hold on.

As I edged around the other side of the building, I sucked in deep gulps of air, trying to steady myself.

I was not back there. I was fine. Lawrence had made it back. All of my family members had made it back. I was fine.

Only I wasn't, and I couldn't fight it. I just needed to stop this.

This was why Lark wasn't mine. I left her standing alone while I came out to deal with my own issues. Because I wasn't strong enough to handle them all.

"Look at you, I can finally get you alone."

Despite the needles digging into my temples, my head shot up at the familiar voice. How had he gotten on the property? With such high security, how had he gotten here?

Holmes stood there, his eyes narrowed, but I saw the

dark circles under them. He'd let his hair grow, way past regulation length, but hell, so was mine. His beard was unkempt, and he wore a t-shirt with holes in the collar, and jeans with tattered knees. He stood there, hands fisted, looking far too skinny.

Holmes had always been muscly, but lean. Strong. That wasn't the man I saw now. I had come back wrong; come back with something I couldn't quite figure out. But Holmes had come back worse. And I hadn't been strong enough to save him, either.

"What do you want, Holmes? How did you get here?"

"You were always an idiot. You never saw what was right in front of you. They didn't kill you when they should have. I'll do it for them." And then Holmes charged at me.

My head throbbed and I was moving too slow, but I still ducked the first punch.

I couldn't duck the second, or the third. And then I couldn't think anymore. I just lashed out and I hit Holmes straight in the face, then the gut, and then people were screaming, but I didn't care.

The explosions were coming, the bullets were flying, and I needed to stop this.

Once and for all.

Chapter Fifteen

Lark

*"The only way to stop loving you is to never love at all.
But then you walked away, and I stayed behind, never
trusting to fall."*

"Heading East" written by Lark Thornbird

I dropped the flowers on the ground at my feet as I ran towards the shout. Others hadn't noticed yet, all focused on the party, the dancing. And whatever was happening hadn't been going on for long, nor was it too loud.

Every time a fist hit flesh, I screamed inside.

Whoever this man was had East by the neck. East

hadn't fought back at first, but now he was, and I needed him to stop.

"Stop! East!" I looked over my shoulder, desperately searching for Trace or somebody from the team. Everybody was working double time, keeping the reception safe, but nobody was doing the same for East.

"Trace!" I practically screamed, and a few people looked over and then Trace was moving, speaking into his mic. Others came with him, but they were still keeping some semblance of quiet, not alerting the Wilders or Bethany. I would not ruin this wedding, but someone needed to help. The music was loud enough that no one heard this, but it wouldn't be too long before someone walked by and it would be noticed.

I ran forward, but then Trace passed me, pulling the man away. My hands shook as I moved to East, but then East scrambled from Jason, hurling himself at the other man, who started screaming obscenities, threatening to kill him.

"Stop, back it down," Trace ordered, and I just stood there between it all, my breath coming in pants.

East's lip was bloody, as were his knuckles, and I was so damn scared.

Not for myself, but someone had hurt East.

"We need to get you to a doctor," I said, as I pulled out the handkerchief that he gave me.

"I'm fine, Lark. I'm fine. You should get out of here."

He kept talking to me, but he wasn't looking at me.

"How the hell did you get on property, Holmes?" he asked, and I froze, recognizing the name.

I turned to see the skinny man with wide eyes full of rage and heartache. This man constantly threatened East. The man that had been through hell, along with East and his team.

"How the hell did he get on property?" East snarled, Jason and the others holding him back.

That's when Eli and Evan showed up, Elliot right behind him. "What the fuck is going on?" Eli asked.

"This man attacked East, from what we can tell."

"How the hell did he get here?" East snapped. "How the hell did you let Holmes on this damn property?"

"This is Holmes?" Elliot asked, wide-eyed. "He was on the list not to be here. What the hell?"

"Well, he's here, and he just attacked East," I said, trying not to get too close to East. I wanted to, I wanted to help him. But he sure as hell didn't want me near him. But he looked so angry, like if the others weren't holding him back he'd lash out again. I didn't blame him, and I wanted some vengeance of my own.

"I know this guy," Jason said with narrowed eyes, as East whipped his head towards him.

"What?" he snapped.

"He worked with the contractor. You guys hired fifteen new guys and he passed every check."

Everyone started talking at once, and I moved to East, risking everything as I put my hand on his arm. "East. They have him. Calm down."

He let out a shaking breath and stared at me, his eyes wild before he blinked it away, looking like himself again.

"I'm fine, Lark. You shouldn't be here. I don't want you to get hurt."

There was a wealth of something in his tone that I didn't want to think about, but I just shook my head.

"I go where you go right now."

"You don't do the hiring, East, the contractor did, and we vetted him." Trace sounded as if he were talking through a mouthful of jagged nails.

"Are you fucking kidding me?" Eli asked, his voice low. "Get him out of my face," he snarled. "We'll handle this." Eli looked at me. "Are you okay? You got this?"

I wondered if he thought I wasn't strong enough to do this. To stand by East during whatever the hell this was. But he was just worried about East.

"We're fine. Let's go, East. Let me clean up that lip."

"You should go back to the wedding."

The wedding. My best friend's wedding. I hoped nobody else had noticed what was going on. You couldn't see us from the venue, but if we weren't careful, it would be a thing. So I pulled on East's hand.

"My cabin's closer. Let's go."

"We've got this," Evan said, glaring at Holmes. I didn't know what was going to happen with the other man, or even what should happen. It wasn't my problem, wasn't my say. I just didn't want it to be East's problem anymore.

Thankfully, East let me drag him to my cabin. I had honestly been prepared for him to go back to Holmes or even go back to his own cabin.

The fact that he came with me told me he was either so far in his head that he couldn't focus, or maybe he was trusting me.

I couldn't hope for the latter though, not when I wasn't sure what the hell was going on between the two of us.

I got East inside, then went straight for the first aid kit and grabbed a clean cloth to wipe his face.

"Sit down and take off your tie. I'll clean you up."

"You don't have to do this, Lark. I should have just gone home. Hell, I fucked up Everett's wedding. Of course, I fucking did."

I turned to him, supplies in hand as I moved forward. "You didn't. No one noticed. And if they did, who cares. You didn't start anything."

"No, it *was* me. I brought this here."

My heart ached for him, but I didn't know what I was supposed to say to make this better. There wasn't any way to do that other than stand here and listen. "You didn't, East. Holmes brought himself here. I don't know what's going on with him, and I'm sorry for it, but it wasn't you. It's not you."

"I should have known." He sighed as I put the ice pack on his lip, his eyes narrowing. "I don't like the fact that you're so good at this."

My lips twitched. "I work with rock stars for a living. I know how to clean up a few punches. But never for myself. My team takes care of me. I take care of me. Especially after."

I didn't have to say it, we both knew. My past wasn't up for discussion, but it was something that was part of me. I wasn't that person anymore, I was stronger, and I had finally learned how to heal.

"We hired how many men? I worked beside most of them, and I didn't know we hired him."

"He hid from you for a reason. And you don't work with each person. I've been here for how long and I don't know everyone who works here."

"Maybe. Or maybe I'm a fucking idiot. It's my job to fix this. To know things." He sighed as I cleaned him up and bandaged his knuckles.

When I finished, I looked at him, trying to see what he needed. I wasn't sure there was anything I could do. "I'm sorry. I'm sorry that this ended your evening."

"Yeah, I ended it before then, don't you remember?" he asked, his voice hollow.

And I did. He had left, walked away and left me standing on the dance floor all alone. Because it had gotten too real. "I didn't like that. You didn't have to do that."

"I'm an asshole. Of course, I did."

He was lying to himself more than me, but then again, people had watched us dance. And soon there would be rumors about a new song with a man that I danced with. I was used to that.

But East wasn't.

And he was right. Maybe he should have walked away like he had. He hadn't asked for any of this.

"Thanks for cleaning me up. I should go."

It felt as if he were ripping out my heart, but I nodded, swallowing hard. "You should go back to the wedding." I wanted to reach out and brush his hair from his face, but I wasn't sure I could touch him and not break down—in heat or in fear, I just didn't know.

"Not looking like this. But you should. It's your friend, your people."

I frowned, confused. "It's your friends and family out there, too."

"Not all of them."

"East, what's going on in that head of yours?"

"Nothing, other than the fact that my past came back today and punched the shit out of me at my brother's wedding. And I danced with you. And I shouldn't have."

Again, that wrench of my heart. "Why? Because people were watching?"

"You know damn well why. You're leaving, we both know that. You don't need more rumors."

The fact that his words went right with my thoughts meant something, but I was still annoyed.

"And you just decided to make that choice for the both of us, to leave me standing there?"

"What else was I supposed to do, Lark?" He got up and began to pace my living room. "I've got to go. I've got to deal with this. And I can't deal with you right now."

It was like a slap, but I was done. I was going to stand up for myself. Damn it.

"No. Don't lash out. If you're done with this, then be done. But don't act like a bitch to me."

He laughed. "Oh, I'm a bitch now?"

"What else are you? You're hurt, I get it. But don't treat me like shit because you don't know what the hell's going on."

"You're leaving. So maybe we should just keep it at that. You're leaving. I'm staying. There's nothing more, Lark. There doesn't need to be."

My throat threatened to close, so I lifted my chin. "Really?"

"Yeah. Really."

He turned then, and froze.

It was like everything was going in slow motion, and I wanted to reach out, to stop him. To do anything but let him walk away. Today had already been too much, and this would be it. He leaned down and picked up my notebook. The one that I kept hidden but had forgotten to put away that morning. Because the final lyrics had come to me. The ones that meant the world. The ones that changed everything.

"Heading East?" He let out a hollow laugh, then turned to me. "I guess I'm not just a distraction."

"It's not what you think."

"Sure. You said you wouldn't though. You said you'd never write a song about me. That I'd never be another checkmark for those who want to make a fucking bingo card."

"I was never going to do anything about it," I claimed, and it was the truth. My heart raced, and I felt like I was going to throw up, but it wasn't what he thought. "This is my work. Yes, I wrote something, but I just needed to get it out of my head. I promised I would never write about you, and I didn't. Not really."

"Well, I'm used to liars. Saw it today. Seems like today's the day for reveals, isn't it? Thanks for everything, Lark. I guess we're done."

He tossed the notebook on my couch and glared at me.

I felt as if I were breaking into a thousand pieces, and I tried to keep up, but I was losing. Losing this, losing him. And maybe I deserved it, but I didn't deserve everything.

"You're hurt. And you're hiding it. I get it, today was a lot. But I never lied. I would never release that song."

"The proof's right there on the couch. It was nice while it lasted, Lark. But I'm not in your world. And the risks that come with it are not for me. It never was. I'll never be that guy. You do what you have to, I don't care anymore. I'm done with this, with hiding. With being. I'm done."

He turned and left, slamming the door behind him.

That slam echoed within my heart, and I didn't realize I was falling to the ground, my dress billowing around me as the tears fell and I broke.

I hadn't meant to write about him. I hadn't meant to fall for him.

But I had, and it was too much. I had known it would

be too much. He had never wanted me like that, and now I had to face the truth.

I wasn't his. I would never be. I was just me.

Chapter Sixteen

East

Bullets flew overhead, smoke slipped into my nostrils, and people screamed. Then the dream shifted and I was drowning, a hand on my face, holding me down.

Another shift. Another breath.

Holmes screaming, a fist to the face.

Another shift. Another breath.

Lawrence holding his children, his wife laughing.

Another shift. Another breath.

Adam lying in a pool of his own blood, our friends dead around him.

Another shift. Another breath.

Eli. Bam. Everett. Bam. Elijah. Bam. Evan. Bam.

Elliot. Screaming. Last.

Joy. Dead. Maddie nearly drowned. Alexis, taken. Kendall, buried.

Everyone, gone.

When I woke up, I couldn't breathe. I clutched my throat, a scream trying to erupt but nothing coming out.

Sweat slicked my skin and I shook, knowing it was from another nightmare.

"Fuck," I growled.

I threw my legs over the edge of the bed and wiped my hands on my thighs. I thought I'd gotten better. I thought I'd gotten through it. I didn't have the same issues my brothers did, I was the healthy one.

I fisted my hands and cursed. I'd forgotten the fight, how could I have forgotten the fucking *fight*?

My knuckles ached, and I stretched them a bit, knowing it probably would've been better if I'd gotten more ice, but I hadn't.

Instead, I had left Lark alone, and brewed in my own misery.

My head ached, and it had nothing to do with the fist to the face, but the third of a bottle of whiskey I had chugged.

I didn't usually drink when things got bad, I hadn't wanted to rely on that as a crutch, but hell, it had been the only thing I could do.

I ignored the calls and visits from my brothers.

They all needed to focus on the wedding and making sure that the place still ran.

After I talked to the cops, making sure that Holmes knew he wasn't allowed on the property anymore, I decided to leave.

I had needed time for myself.

I had walked away from everything, from who I had thought I could be, and from Lark.

Dammit.

I wasn't even mad about the song. It was such a silly fucking thing to be mad about. It was just an easy excuse, and I had taken it. I could have blamed myself, could have blamed everything on Holmes and walked away then. No, it had been easier to put the blame on her so I wouldn't have to take responsibility for my own actions.

I was the asshole I had claimed to be, and there was no going back.

But now Lark would leave, and I wouldn't have to wait for her to leave. She would just be gone, and I would be done.

Finally, I could move on and live in my little world where nothing mattered.

I got out of bed and limped my way to the shower.

I turned the tap to cold, knowing the ice would help.

I had done the worst thing I could have possibly done.

I had fallen in love with Lark.

And I didn't know what I was supposed to do about it. I had hurt her before she could hurt me—and what a piece of shit that made me. I slid my head underneath the water, letting the ice-cold water slam into my system. It was like dipping into an ice bath, but I kept going, my hands on the tile, tilting my head so that way I could get more of it. I just needed to wake up and get back to work.

Find a normal that made sense.

The spa would be opening soon, and then we would break ground on the next project. Trace was going to move onto the compound and settle in and help us make things work.

We had things to do, and me being in my own head wasn't going to help.

I had been better. Therapy helped. Moving here with my brothers helped.

And here I was, breaking again. Because I had left her.

Just like Holmes said I had left the others.

I paused, letting out a hollow laugh at that twisted thought.

Well, it seems I was the product of my own demise. Lucky me.

I was done feeling sorry for myself; I quickly finished washing up, then wrapped a towel around my waist so I could head into my bedroom and find something to wear.

I had things to do, and wallowing in my own self-pity wasn't going to help. I should've known I wouldn't be alone though. Everyone had a damn key to my house. I was never alone. Even when I needed to be.

Eli leaned against the doorway, while Elliot sat on the small chair in the corner, shaking his head. They both looked tired, not like they'd been at a family wedding the night before.

Sometimes it was hard to remember that we had moved here for a reason. That we had all been falling and fading and not able to save ourselves.

We wouldn't have been who we were if we hadn't come together and made this place our own. I didn't want to think about what we would've become without each other.

And here I was kind of fucking it up.

"You look like hell," Eli said, shaking his head.

"Thank you for breaking into my house to tell me that."

"I'm just telling you the truth. You look like hell. I should be with my kid, you know. I should have been able to sleep in, sleep with my wife, and then hang out with Kylie for the morning. But no, not today. Instead, I'm here having to deal with your sorry ass, because you won't deal with it yourself."

Elliot barked out a laugh from his chair as he leaned

back, crossed his ankle over his knee, and rested his hands over his stomach. "See, that's an older brother for you. An older brother who was up late last night with a kid who ate too many sweets and decided to throw it up all over Alexis. Because parents get to deal with things like that. And he's had to parent us on top of that, even when we were fully grown."

Alarmed, I immediately turned to Eli. "Is Kylie okay? Do you need me to do something?"

"Well, at least you're not completely lost to us," Eli said. "Your niece is fine." He pinched the bridge of his nose, sighed. "She and the twins decided to get into the extra cake Kendall had made for the event. Well, they're Wilders, we should expect this type of things," he said with a growl.

The idea of Reese, Cassie, and Kylie climbing over everything in order to eat extra cake made me want to smile. I loved all my nieces and nephews.

They were our family, and I didn't get to spend as much time with them as I wanted to, mostly because I'd been in my own world. I needed to be better about that. But now that I had fucked up everything with Lark, I would. I'd find all the time in the world. Because I didn't have anything else.

"What about Lexington and Silas?" I asked, mentioning Eliza's kids. "Did they make a ruckus too?"

"They were the ones on watch, and only missed out on getting the cake because we caught them. So Eliza didn't have to clean up puke like the rest of us did."

I winced. "I'm sorry."

"It's fine. It happens. Alexis is cuddling with Kylie for the day, and I'm going to head back. That is, after you and I talk about whatever the hell is going on in your head."

I froze, that familiar feeling of not being enough coming back. "It's nothing."

"It's everything," Elliot replied.

"You got in a fight on the property. Our property. Where anyone could have seen. Luckily the guests didn't seem to have noticed. It didn't make the news, and no one seems to have caught wind, but the cops had to come here discreetly."

"I was there for that," I snapped, and let out a breath. "I'm sorry. I'm sorry for all of this."

"That part isn't your fault," Eli put in, and Elliot nodded.

"You were just telling me it was," I shouted back.

"I was just adding on to whatever the hell happened yesterday. You got in a fight because that man attacked you. He's been threatening you for how long, and now he's physically attacked you? No. It's not your fault. But we're brothers, we come to each other when we need things."

I let out a hollow laugh, no lick of humor in it. "That's rich coming from you," I snarled at Elliot, who just froze and shook his head.

"We're not talking about me."

"We will, but first we deal with this one," Eli ordered.

Elliot shut down in front of us, and I was sad for it, but if I was going down apparently I was taking my brothers with me.

"What do you want me to do?" I asked. "I talked to the police. Nobody caught wind of it. Holmes is gone. You say it's not my fault, so what do you want me to do?"

"I want you to talk about it." Eli threw up his hands. "I want you to get some help. Because you're drowning, East. And I can't help you. I have had to watch all of my brothers drown and there's nothing I can do. We lost Mom and Dad, and now I'm losing all of you one by one. I can't lose you again. Let us help you."

I rubbed my eyes, shaking my head. I sat on the edge of the bed in a towel, feeling far more bare than that. "There's nothing you can do. I'm fixing it. Figuring it out."

"Are you going to go talk to Dr. Channing again?" Elliot asked.

"I guess. I was doing better."

"It doesn't just go away. People like Holmes bring it back, but we're always here to help," Eli added.

"Yeah. I'll talk with Dr. Channing. I'll do whatever.

I'll get back to work. I have a shit ton to do on my schedule, and if you'll let me, I'll go visit Kylie and make sure she's okay. Be a better uncle than I've been." I was so focused on keeping the place working and ignoring my own problems, I felt like I was ignoring everyone else.

"I'm never going to keep you away from my kid, East. You're my brother. Now, what are you going to do about Lark?" Eli asked.

I shook my head. "Nothing. It's over. That's over." I repeated.

"Well, then you're really not going to want to look at social media right now," Elliot replied.

My head shot up and I glared. "What the fuck are you talking about?"

"It seems like somebody caught your dance. It was bound to happen. You marking your territory like that in front of everyone, and then walking away. Right now, it's just speculations about another Wilder falling, and about Lark's new album. They're speculating, she's not commenting, and neither are you."

"Fuck," I growled. This was the one thing I hadn't wanted to happen, but nothing I wanted these days was actually working out for me.

"What are you going to do about Lark?"

"There is no me and Lark. It's over. She can go back to

her regular life, and this will fade. She's used to people speculating, and it sucks, but she'll get over it. And they'll forget me. I'm just here. I'm not meant for anything more."

"That's a cop-out and you know it," Eli added.

"It's the truth. I don't know what more you want from me. I'm done. She's done. We weren't meant to work out. We're not meant for that. Yeah, we had a good time together, but I never even took her out for a fucking date," I snarled, as they stared at me.

Everything started to hit me at once, and I cursed. "We had nothing but sex. Yeah, we had fun, but I never took her off this fucking property. We had weeks here, where she hid from the world and I was just her distraction and that's fine. But now she's going back and she can move on and do what she needs to, and I'll stay here, go to Dr. Channing, whatever. But I don't want to talk about Lark anymore. It's over, it's done and I'm just fucking tired of it."

Elliot stared at me, wide-eyed, while Eli studied my face. I hated the fact that they could read me so well, that they would know exactly what I was feeling even if I didn't.

"I've just got to go talk with Trace," I said as I stood up, hand on my towel. "If you want to stand here while I get dressed, go for it. If not, I could use some privacy."

"You pushing us out like this isn't going to help things," Eli said softly.

"I'm not sure what else I'm supposed to do. I've got work to do, I've got family to be with, and I've got a life to live. Lark isn't part of it. We were never anything more than sex, Eli. I don't think there needs to be anything else."

I dropped the towel and got dressed. My brothers sighed and left me with my own thoughts.

I had things to do. I needed to talk with Trace, I needed to make plans. I needed to figure out whatever the hell was going on with Holmes.

Lark wasn't part of any of it.

We hadn't been dating, I hadn't been hers. We had a few stolen moments. That was it. Once I got that through my head, I'd get over it.

At least I hoped to hell I would.

Chapter Seventeen

Lark

"*I am enough. I am my own. I am forever. I am strong. I am enough. But I'm never yours.*"

"*Broken" written by Lark Thornbird*

It felt as if somebody had ripped out my heart and stepped on it. An apt description, a metaphor countless others had used, and I was out of words to make myself unique. He had overreacted, and yet a small part of me knew he had done that because he needed to run away. To push me away.

Well, he succeeded. I was done. I had dealt with people not respecting me, not respecting my work, and not loving me enough to stay before. I would deal with it again now, by not doing anything at all when it came to him. I would walk away, and never look back.

I finished packing the last of my shoes and let out a hollow laugh.

Oh, that was rich. Because of course I would have to come back. Why? Because my best friend was part of his family. Bethany and Everett might be on their honeymoon as of this morning, and had no idea that my life was irrevocably altered, but they were his family. And Bethany was mine. I wasn't going to be able to walk away from this and never look back. Because he would always be here.

I was going to have to be the stronger person and get over it—and him.

I still couldn't quite believe he had reacted as he had, but I shouldn't have been surprised. He had been looking for a way out the first time we had been together. So why did I think that anything would be different once things might have gotten serious?

I angrily stuffed my toiletries in my suitcase, then zipped everything up, practically slamming the lid closed as I did.

"Well, fuck him. Fuck it all. I'm done. I'm going to get over this."

Because fuck him.

Only, it wasn't really like that, was it?

Not when I felt like everything was breaking inside and I wasn't going to be able to stop.

I was done. I would write a breakup song that had nothing to do with him and would be an abstract thing for the narrative, and everything would be fine.

Of course, then I remembered that people already thought that I was with that mystery Wilder, so that's something else I'd have to deal with. But I would ignore it. I would deal like I always did.

I had meandered my way through multiple fictional breakups, I could deal with this one, too.

I set my bag near the front door, ready for the car service to come pick me up. I was tired, oh so tired, but it didn't matter. I just had to get through the day. Someone knocked on the door as soon as I thought that. I froze, oddly worried—and hopeful—it would be him.

But no, it wouldn't be.

I didn't want to feel that hope that it could be him. I didn't want it to *not* be him either.

"Lark? It's me."

Oddly disappointed and yet relieved at the sound of Elliot's voice, I opened the door to see East's brother standing there, his hands in his pockets, looking sad yet determined.

I didn't know if I liked that mixture in his eyes. "Is everyone okay?"

Elliot let out a sigh. "It worries me that that's the first thing you ask since we have been through so much stress recently, that you even have to worry if we're okay."

I winced and shook my head. "I'm sorry."

"Don't be. That's not your fault. If anything, you've been a model guest. You haven't brought the issues. We seem to be doing that ourselves."

"It's not you. It's the rest of the world." I thought of East, the anger in his eyes. "Okay, maybe it's some of you."

Elliot winced again. "Well. I was going to ask how you're feeling, but since I hear that tone, I guess I know."

"I don't really have time to talk about anything, Elliot. I have to go back to the rest of my life."

"I guess you've been away from it for a while now."

I gestured for him to come inside, not in the mood to have this conversation while he was still on my porch.

"I've been gone far too long. I got some work done while I was here, but this isn't my life. I was reminded of that this week. I have people who rely on me, a life to live, and work to do. So that's what I'll do."

"My brother is an asshole."

I let out a soft laugh. "Maybe. But I'm the one who let myself believe otherwise. Or maybe I was just deluded."

"You're not deluded at all. I see the way he looks at you. He has feelings for you. You guys are good for each other."

I blinked before shaking my head. "*Did* anyone ever see us together? No. Because we were secret. We were better at hiding everything. We weren't even in a real relationship. I get that. And I'm fine. We didn't have what I thought we did. And it took me too long to figure that out."

"You had more than that," Elliot added.

"Did we? We just hung out a few times. We talked to one another. We ate together. But we weren't a couple. And I get that. I'm fine."

Elliot stared at me for so long I was afraid he saw too much. But maybe I needed him to.

"You're not fine," Elliot said softly.

I stared at him and didn't know what to say. I had been living in a bubble, something far removed from who I was, so it made sense that East and I wouldn't work. Because while he got to know the real me, he hadn't gotten to know the me outside of these walls. And East would never leave. He would never want to be out there. "No, I'm not," I said truthfully. "But not everybody gets a Wilder."

Elliot's eyes softened, and he shook his head. "I don't know what happened, why East is hurting the way he is and why you seem to be doing the same, but I'm sorry for it. And I wish there was something I could do."

"There's nothing. But thank you. I'm leaving soon. I

have to go to work. I have to sing and do what I love and put this behind me. I'll come back—you know that. For Bethany, for you guys. I'll have to come back, I'll have to face him and pretend that this never happened. If you could let me do that, that would be great."

Elliot started to say something, but he just opened his arms and hugged me tightly. I held him back so tight I was afraid we were both going to stop breathing, but I didn't cry, I didn't let the tears fall. Instead, I leaned on him, letting myself just be for once, and then I pulled away, and he left without another word.

I was good at writing love, at writing heartbreak. But I was not good at loving. That was hard to understand, but I was there. And I would finally take it to heart.

I stuffed everything else into my purse, then cursed when I noticed the note I hadn't dealt with yet. I needed to give it to him. I should have given it to Elliot. It wasn't just for East.

But it was important.

I picked up the notebook, slid the envelope inside, and made my way to East's cabin. I had written notes about the spa for the Wilders, though I didn't think they really needed me. Maybe it had just been a ploy to get us together, to keep East busy. I didn't know the realities of it, but in the end it didn't matter. It had worked for a moment, but then not at all.

I stopped by East's cabin and had to figure out what to do. His door was locked, but I didn't want to leave.

I slid the notebook with his song, the one I was never going to release, but was etched into my heart, on the porch, with his note buried inside. There wasn't anything of me in the note, just ideas from my parents, just business.

I hadn't needed to put myself in the note. I was already in the song.

I sighed and slid my hands into my pockets, cursing when I realized I left my phone in my purse.

I needed to head back. I had a life to live, and it wasn't here. I had spoken the truth when I had told Elliot that not everybody got a Wilder. Bethany got hers, I didn't get mine. I would move on. I was done. I worked hard. I was a writer; it was part of who I was. I wouldn't be sad. I'd be angry. Anger would help.

So fuck him, and fuck him for hurting me.

I walked around the back of his cabin to head back to mine, and passed his work cabin where all of his tools and things for his work were stored. I didn't hear him inside, so thankfully I wasn't going to have to face him.

"He doesn't deserve you."

I whirled at the voice, recognizing it too late. The man moved forward, close enough I could feel the heat of his breath on my neck. I put my hands above my face as the guy slammed a rock towards me. Shocking pain slid up my shoulder as he missed my face, bile rising up my throat at the agony slamming into my body.

I hit the ground, my head going dizzy as he pulled my hair. I screamed, kicking out, trying to do something, hoping someone would hear me. He had his hand on my mouth and I couldn't bite down. He kicked me again and I squirmed, trying to move. But he slammed my head against the ground and I nearly threw up, everything going fuzzy. I couldn't focus. I couldn't move.

He tossed me inside the building, and that's when I smelled smoke.

"He's going to understand. He's going to understand." Holmes slammed the door as flames licked at the back of the cabin. I screamed, trying to get out. *Holmes had just locked me inside a burning cabin.* I coughed, smoke filling my lungs. Holmes had secured the windows so I couldn't get out. The doorknob wouldn't move and when Holmes kicked at the door from the other side and shouted, I realized he'd jammed it somehow. I wasn't getting out that way, but I couldn't move past the flames on the other side to get to the backdoor. I looked for another way out, but there was nothing.

Just my own screams.

Chapter Eighteen

East

I ducked the punch to my face and went in with an uppercut. Trace laughed as he staggered back, rubbing his jaw.

"I thought you weren't going full force."

I rolled my eyes. "We're boxing. I'm not going to hit you with all my strength."

"Damn thankful for that, because I think one of my teeth is loose."

I winced. "Sorry."

"Don't be. You've got a lot of rage, though I'd love to figure out why."

"No reason," I lied.

"Well, if I'm going to get out my non-rage on you, beware, I'm in a fucking mood too."

"You can hit harder than me with just your pinky, so maybe don't use all of your strength."

I dodged to the right, moved to the left, thankful that we were wearing as much safety gear as possible.

I didn't need to be bruised and bloody more than I already was. My knuckles hurt from the fight with Holmes, but there wasn't anything I could do.

I just needed to fight, to get it out, and Trace was here. I didn't know how much longer he would be here before he had to leave to finish up his affairs with his former job. But then he would be a full-time member of the Wilders, and it would be good to have him here. Good to fight with somebody, to get out this rage.

"So, you want to talk about it?" Trace asked as we cleaned up and chugged water.

I flipped him off. "I just told you I didn't."

"I don't know, sounds like you do."

"What? The cops and you escorted Holmes off the property, and we couldn't press charges for trespassing, so he's still out there, annoyed as fuck."

"You're going to use that restraining order?"

"Getting one." I sighed. "My brothers are smarter than me sometimes, I should have already had one."

"Maybe. Or maybe letters like that wouldn't have done much. But you're going to keep your family safe.

Keep yourself safe. But I don't think it's just Holmes on your mind. Your other friend's gone, headed home with his family. He's safe. Are you two going to talk?" he asked.

I'd already told Trace everything. It was odd to think we had clicked as friends as quickly as we had, but Trace understood things. Maybe because Trace had seen more than I ever would. He didn't share as much as I did. The other man and my family tended to pull things out of me.

"I need to head back in to work. This was my lunch break," I said in lieu of answering, and Trace rolled his eyes.

"Fine. Don't talk about it."

"I'll talk as soon as you talk to me about your personal life, how's that?"

Trace shrugged. "Touché. Though you probably should eat something."

I shrugged this time. I hadn't been in the mood to eat and wasn't sure I would be for a bit. Every time I thought about it, about what I had said to Lark, how I had treated her, I felt sick.

"Come on, I need to head out."

"Sounds good."

My phone buzzed, as the alarms went off with the admin alert. "Fuck, that's the fire alarm."

"I'm on it, calling security."

"It's my cabin!" I called out as I looked at the security alerts, and then Trace and I were running, seeing smoke billowing from my cabin, stinging my eyes.

Eli was there already, pushing back a few guests. I cursed, watching my work cabin go up into flames.

"Jesus," I whispered. Had I left something on? Had some electrical wiring gone bad?

And then the most chilling thing I'd ever heard in my life hit my ear, and it felt as if the world was fading away.

"Was that a fucking scream?" Trace asked.

I looked towards my home and saw the notebooks sitting there. Chills crept up my spine. I knew those notebooks, that writing. But she wasn't here. Wasn't standing outside. But I knew that voice.

Lark was in there. In my cabin.

"Lark!" I screamed as I moved towards the flames.

"Jesus, you're going to kill yourself," Trace shouted as he pulled me back, Evan and Elliot coming up right behind me.

"You think Lark's in there?"

As someone pounded on the door from the other side, I didn't think, I just rammed my body into the door, noticing that someone had done something to it so it wouldn't open.

"Somebody locked her in there. Lark! I'm coming. Stand back."

"East!" she called out, and then she coughed, her words fading.

"I've got to get her."

The sound of gunshots came back to me, a memory: my men screaming for me, Lawrence being pulled away, Holmes shouting.

This was Holmes. It had to be.

Someone had sabotaged my cabin and set it on fire, while locking Lark in there. Numbness settled in and I let it. My hands shook, but I kept going as the others tried to put the fire out.

"I'm coming, Lark!"

"Hurry!"

The others were shouting, but I could only hear Lark. *My* Lark.

We kicked at the door, trying to break through windows that had been sabotaged somehow. And then I was inside, smashing the door in, and Lark was at my feet. She looked up at me, struggling to stand, a wet rag in front of her face. She was covered in blood, her eyes red and wide.

I picked her up without thinking, ignoring the flames as they licked at me from behind. Lark was as far away from the fire as possible, but she was still surrounded by smoke. I didn't know if she was hurt, didn't know what was happening. I didn't know if she was burned or if she had breathed too much of the smoke. I could hear others shouting, saying that the windows had been jammed shut.

Someone had tried to kill her, had done this on purpose.

I carried Lark out into the middle of the walkway, ignoring the others as they came forward.

"Are you okay?"

She blinked at me. "I'm fine. It was Holmes," she coughed.

When I pushed her hair back from her face, I noticed the slight red tinges on a few parts of her skin, the blood covering her shirt and side.

That fucker had hurt her. And her beautiful voice, she had a rasp to it now from having inhaled so much smoke. She could have died, she could still die, and that damn haunting injury came back, a rearing force that wanted to remove everything. I had to push through. I had to breathe through the panic like I had been taught.

Lark needed me. I held her, and I ignored the screams echoing in my head.

My brothers were there, as were others, and when the firemen came, the paramedics right on their heels, I let them take Lark.

Only first I pressed my lips to her forehead, and she rubbed her hand on my chest.

226

"I'm fine, East. I'm fine. He didn't really hurt me." Her voice sounded so shaky, yet so far away. "I...I'm okay."

My breaths came in pants, and I tried to work through the sound of a train echoing through my ears. Because my past had nearly killed Lark...and I had no idea if she was truly okay now.

The paramedics pulled her from me, and she gave me one last look before her eyes closed. This was my fault. I'd left her, had hurt her. And now my past had almost killed her.

Alexis got in the back of the ambulance with her, and I stood there, by the remnants of my cabin, as people worked to put out the fire and my family worked to calm the guests.

"How the hell did he get back on our property?" It was the only thing I could say. I'd let her go away again. Because it was for the best. She was safer without me.

Trace stood by me, hands fisted. "He paid the new guy we hired. The guy I had vetted. I'm staying here full-time. I'm fixing this. I'm not letting this happen again."

I wanted to lash out, to rage, only I didn't. It wasn't Trace's fault. It was mine. I had brought Holmes into this. I had left Lark alone.

I would fix this. I wasn't sure how, but I would. Lark was hurt because of me. But she wasn't mine to heal. Yet, I knew I needed to fix this. I needed to do something.

I would make this up to her.

Because I had almost lost her.

I loved her. *I fucking loved Lark,* and I hadn't had the balls to say it. I was almost too late.

"What are you going to do?" Evan asked, his voice low.

I turned to him, my eyes wide. "I need to fix this."

"Go to her. Help her."

"I don't know if I have the right..."

He didn't say anything in answer, and I didn't blame him. I didn't know what I wanted him to say.

Hours later, we stood and watched the burned corpse of my shed. My main cabin and the rest of the property were safe. It hadn't spread. But it had still been a shock.

"I am damn tired of our family getting hurt," Eli murmured.

"Beyond tired," Evan added.

"And it's not just you this time," Elliot put in as he looked at me.

I nodded tightly as Elijah gripped my shoulder. He cleared his throat, looking as tired as we were. "For some reason, though we got out when we did, trying to come together to protect ourselves, the world doesn't see it this way. So, we're going to circle back, tighten the reins, do all the other metaphors there are to keep us safe."

I nodded, agreeing with him. "And we're going to protect our family. *All* of our family. Because this isn't happening again," I said, hoping they understood the meaning. Hoping they understood that Lark was my family, even though I had pushed her away.

I still held her notebook in my hand, her lyrics had been for me, a part of her soul that I had almost broken. Or perhaps I already had.

"I don't want this to happen to us again. I don't want this to mar who we are."

"It might for a while," Eli added. "Because this is our property and we're not keeping the guests safe. But we will find a way. We have to. But you're right, I'm damn tired of this. We're not going to let it happen again."

We all nodded, and in a sense, we made a pact.

We were the Wilder brothers, and our family was growing day by day, and that meant we had to protect them. No matter the cost, no matter the pain. But we had each other, and we weren't going to let the world hurt us again. That meant first I had to go back and make sure I healed the person that I had hurt in the process.

Lark deserved far more than me, but maybe I would find a way for her to believe me. To forgive me.

I loved her, and now I needed to prove it, not only to

myself, but to the woman who deserved far more than a man who almost broke her.

Only, now I needed to figure out how to make it happen.

Chapter Nineteen

Lark

"I lost you before I could find myself. But now I know the woman in the mirror...and I'll always know you could have been there."

"Lost and Found" written by Lark Thornbird

It had been two weeks since the fire, since I had walked away because there had been nothing left for either of us.

Then again, he had walked away first, and I had to live with that.

I loved East Wilder, and I was the stupidest person ever to think that it would be okay to do.

We had both promised each other at first that we

wouldn't fall in love. And I was the fool who had done it anyway.

He hadn't even called. He hadn't reached out, other than through his family to make sure I was fine.

The second-degree burns on my hip and my leg would heal. I had respiratory therapy to ensure that the smoke that I inhaled wouldn't hurt my vocal cords permanently. I was still a singer-songwriter. I needed my voice for a living. I used my voice as a window to my soul so I could bear witness to the feelings and moments and memories I held. East wouldn't understand that.

He had saved my life, had gone through the hell of his past and the fires that burned in his dreams in order to save me.

And yet I wasn't his.

He had made sure of that, and I wasn't strong enough to bear to see him again.

I couldn't bear the pity in his eyes when he looked at me.

I just had to remember that I wasn't his.

And I would be okay.

I stood in my house in LA, packing boxes all around me. Like Bethany had wanted, I was moving. For now, I'd be renting a larger home in a gated community, one away from the paparazzi. My realtor was on the hunt for something more permanent, but for now I would be renting from an Oscar Award-winning actor who had another home in Montana. They only used this one for award ceremonies when they were in town. I would stay there for three months, and maybe longer if I couldn't find something. But I would find something permanent eventually.

At least that's what everyone told me.

It was so odd that part of me had thought I'd be moving to Texas, that I'd follow in Bethany's footsteps and make a home with the Wilders.

He didn't love me.

I had the news on in the background, not for celebrity gossip, but because I needed to see what was happening outside of my own world. I needed to know that I could touch reality, and live in it, and not wallow in my own torment.

The news was already onto the next celebrity scandal anyway—a cheating spouse with a secret child.

Nobody really cared even after only two weeks that Lark Thornbird had almost died in a fire. Nobody had put it together that it was East that had saved me. No, they just called it the Wilder Curse. That another near-tragedy had happened on the Wilder property.

Even celebrity news hadn't been the only thing to help take the spotlight off the fire that had nearly taken my life, that had taken East from me in every other way.

Bethany and Everett had done something I never thought they would ever do—they released a picture from their honeymoon, just a small photo on social media of the two of them in their bathing suits, smiling and laughing at one another in the sunset. They'd only done it to keep the Wilder fire and curse and my pain out of the news.

I understood why they did it, and I hated the fact that they had done it at all. It wasn't their fault. They hadn't been part of that fire, but they had used their own personal and private business to help their family. And me.

A family I would never be part of, because East didn't understand me or trust me.

And how was I supposed to trust him at all?

I sighed and went to my notebooks, the ones that I would pack up last before the move.

My fingers trailed along the top of the notebook, and I sighed.

I had finished the song. I'd even named it. "Heading East." Cheesy if you understood who it was about, mysterious if you didn't.

I would never publish this song. I would never allow the world to see that part of me.

I couldn't.

They say the hardest part is taking the fall.

But they never tell you the risk that comes by saying nothing at all.

I promised myself I'd never let him see.

Then the world lied to both of us, and I can't make him believe.

It's odd that I had written that before I had truly fallen in love with East. Before everything happened and changed us. The lyrics now had a new meaning. And since those lyrics were repeated twice in the song itself, the first time they were spoken was of a different Lark, a different way that Lark felt about East.

Nobody would know that in the second chorus those words were of a broken woman. One that had finally fallen in love. Who could write hundreds of lyrics about that feeling, and yet would never feel it.

I had made a promise. A promise he already thought I had broken.

And I had nothing left.

The doorbell rang and I frowned, looking at the read-out. Jason had come with me for the first few days for my security but had headed back to Texas because his wife had gone into labor. He had made it for the birth of their baby, and I was happy for that. I wouldn't have been able to forgive myself if he had missed it because of me. But now, I had other security that were on the grounds of the small house I owned for a little while longer.

No one had called me to tell me who it was, so it had to be someone I knew. I didn't want to see them, whoever it was. I sighed and frowned when I looked at the screen.

Why did it have to be him?

I didn't want it to be him.

I opened the door and East stood there. I didn't know what I was supposed to say. He stood on my front porch, looking far too big and growly for my tiny bungalow.

He'd brushed his hair back from his face, but a few pieces still slid over his forehead. I knew that in a matter of moments he'd probably brush it away again. I swallowed hard, sucking in deep breaths as I stared at him. His beard was longer than before—he hadn't bothered to trim it over the last two weeks. He had dark circles under his eyes, and he still had scrapes across his knuckles. He had burnt his arm, but now it was covered in a long-sleeved olive-green Henley. Bethany and the others had told me that he was fine, that he would heal quickly, and he was helping rebuild. He was currently living with Elliot, the two of them sharing a medium-sized cabin, though Elliot said East didn't talk.

Was he speaking to anyone? He should. He needed to talk it out. I had just been in the way, that other man had come to hurt *him*, not me directly.

"I was afraid you weren't going to open the door."

"I wasn't sure I would. Why are you here?"

The last sentence sounded a bit more accusatory than I meant. But then again, I didn't understand why he was here at all. He wasn't back in Texas, and nobody warned me he was coming.

"May I come inside? I don't know if anyone's seen me yet, but I don't think you want people to see me at your front door."

I swallowed hard and moved in quickly, knowing he was right. The security team hadn't mentioned seeing photographers today, but the photographers were sneaky.

"Why didn't anyone tell me you were coming?" I asked quickly, so damn confused about why he was here. I was just starting to breathe again, knowing that I would never be his and he would never be mine, and now he was here in my space and it was all too much.

"I didn't tell them," he said with a laugh, only it rang hollow.

"You left? You just left without letting them know?"

"I told Trace," he said, meeting my gaze. "So that way he could tell the others after I was gone. It was chicken shit of me, but I didn't really know what to say to them. Sorry that I'm a fucking idiot and I need to grovel, so here I am."

I blinked, trying to catch up with exactly what he was saying. "You want to grovel?"

237

He looked at me, his eyes so sad. I could write so much about those eyes, but I wouldn't.

"I left you. You know that, right? Of course you know that. I was so damn up in my head and selfish that I walked away just because you were doing what comes naturally to you. I should have trusted you and I didn't. And because I didn't, you were alone where Holmes could hurt you. He hurt you, and there's nothing I can do to go back and fix that. And I will never forgive myself for that. It's just one thing to add to the pile of shit that I've done that I'm sorry for. I'm so sorry that you were hurt because of me."

I held up my hands before he could continue and shook my head. "No. You don't get to blame yourself for that. That was on him. Holmes did that. You had nothing to do with that."

"He was after me."

"Because he felt guilty. You were hurt over there. You still have scars, and I have touched every single one of them. At least the ones that are on the outside. And I know you have guilt for surviving. But you weren't thriving. You were slowly finding your way with your brothers, and maybe, if I let myself believe, me too."

"Lark, of course you too."

I moved on quickly from that, not wanting to latch

onto that. I couldn't. "It wasn't your fault. I don't blame you."

"But you walked away too. You left right after. You left me, just like I left you."

I let out a hollow laugh, wanting to cry or rail. But no, he was here. He took this step so we could talk it out. Because we damn well hadn't done it before.

"I work hard at what I do. Writing is my work. But I wouldn't have hurt you. No matter what I wrote down because I needed to, I wouldn't have hurt you. And maybe it's selfish of me for even putting those lyrics down, but it's part of me, *just* for me. And you hurt me. Not because of what happened with Holmes. But because you didn't trust me. And I thought we had finally figured out that we could trust each other."

"I'm so fucking sorry. Lark, I know that. I realize that. And I have no idea why I was so worried that you were just going to do something like that. Because I know you wouldn't. You haven't for anyone else, and even if you did, so the fuck what?"

I froze, confused. "What?"

"You're a singer. It's what you do for a living. I am the idiot who put a stamp of disapproval on it the first time we slept together. I'm the one who drew the line in the sand, and I was so stuck on what I was feeling for you that I clung to that line, even though it didn't make any rational sense and it didn't fucking matter. You are brilliant at what you do. That song, from the glimpse I read? It was beautiful. I have no idea how you can put so much feeling into your music, but every time I hear you sing? I can breathe again."

If he would've slapped me, it wouldn't have shocked me more, and I just stared at him, blinking. "What are you saying?" I asked, confused.

"I'm saying that I'm in love with you. I love you so damn much. And I wouldn't let myself believe it because I knew you were leaving. I knew you would go back into this world that is not mine, one that I'm not sure I know how to even begin to be part of. I'm still trying to get my head out of my ass and figure out how to heal and to live like a fucking Wilder. And you are Lark Fucking Thornbird. You're amazing. And I was so damn worried that as soon as you wrote your words that you would leave, that I thought in my head that maybe if you didn't write them it wouldn't happen. It makes no logical sense, but there's nothing logical about the way that I feel about you. I love you. And I'm so damn sorry that I hurt you. That I left. That I made you leave. But I love you, Lark. And no matter what I have to do, I will try to earn your trust again. To earn the words that you wrote. And I hope to hell you write a thousand more songs about us. That I have the ability to sit and watch you write and thrive. So let me be that person. Let me be your person. Let me just be yours."

He stood in front of me as tears slid down my cheeks, and I just stared at him, so utterly confused and enraptured that I had no words. Me, the queen of them, had nothing.

"You're the poet, I love you so much, East. I was so afraid to write down everything that I felt because if I did then it was real and then I wouldn't be able to walk away."

"Don't walk away. Walk with me. Or whatever the hell you want to say. You're the one who could write it better."

"I don't know, you were doing a pretty damn good job."

"I'm sorry for hurting you. For making you feel that you weren't worth my feelings. I'm sorry for so damn much."

"We have a lot to be sorry about, but I want more. I have no idea what this means or what we're going to do, but I love you, too. I love you so damn much."

He kissed me. I smiled into him, and kissed him back, knowing that he was my East, and I loved him so damn much it was so hard to even wrap my mind around it.

"I know that you're moving, Bethany told me. To a safer place and I'm damn well glad about it. But I'm putting my roots down with my family, and I don't know, if you have time, I'd love for you to stay. With me. Here, there, I don't care. But stay. Be mine, Lark. Let us figure this out together."

"Anywhere you are, I'll stay. And we'll figure it out together."

He kissed me again. It was just the beginning. Later, a long while later, naked and pressed together, I breathed in his scent, held him close, and we spoke of things that we should have a long while ago.

I didn't know what would happen next, what we would do with one another. But I knew that I wanted him to be my husband, to be my future. We were just beginning, just figuring out our path. And it wasn't going to be easy, not with the paparazzi, and the media who wanted to know who we were and what we were doing. But we would persevere. And I would write my songs.

And, for the first time in a long time, they would be real.

I wouldn't be the girl who wrote about her ex-boyfriends.

I would be the woman who wrote about her man.

Her only. And her forever.

Chapter Twenty

East

Light slid in through the blinds and I blinked my eyes open, aware that it was the first time in a long time that I hadn't woken in a cold sweat because of a nightmare, or from my alarm. Instead, I was content. Content for the first time in far too long. And it didn't even feel real.

I sighed and tightened my arms around Lark, wondering how this was my new normal.

When she rubbed herself against me, I groaned and remembered that we were both naked.

I slid my hand from her hip to between her legs, and she opened for me. She still had that deep breathing of someone asleep, but she trusted me here. However, I was going to wake her up. She needed to be present for this, I needed her for this. Just like I knew that she needed me.

What a novel concept.

I licked across her shoulder, biting down gently. She let out a contented sigh.

"Good morning."

"Good morning." And when I slid my fingers deep inside her, she moaned, so guttural it went straight to my cock.

"Oh, good morning indeed."

"You're so warm and wet, all perfect for me."

"It's hard to breathe with you around. I feel like I'm always wet just thinking of you."

I closed my eyes and counted to ten. She didn't want me to come on her ass. But with just her words, it was hard for me not to go off right then and there.

"Damn. You say the sweetest things."

"Considering I feel the lead pipe on my ass behind me, I guess I'm not the only one that's ready for this morning."

I grinned. "Damn straight. Now, where was I?" I asked softly, before working my way deep inside her, playing with her clit, loving the way that her pussy flooded around my fingers.

"If you don't stop that, I'm going to come right on your hand. And you haven't even kissed me."

I continued to move, gently at first, then a bit more, as she arched in front of me.

I did what I did best and continued that movement, wanting—needing—her to come.

And when she did, I tilted her chin up so I could capture her mouth.

She kept moving, riding my hands, so I kept the motion up, knowing that no matter what we did, this was just for us, a way we could wake up every morning until the end of our days.

When she finally stopped shaking, she tilted her hips, so I slid my fingers out of her and entered her from behind. She was so wet and slick. We had been tested, and she was on birth control, so I was able to go bare inside her.

Finally, I could go bare inside my woman.

She was hot and wet and it was the best damn feeling I'd ever had in my life.

I was so damn lucky.

She met me slow thrust for slow thrust. I kissed along her jaw, loving the way that she blushed in front of me. She had her hand around my back, gripping me, as I slid my hand from between her legs to her breasts. Her nipples pebbled against my palm, and I kept moving, aching, wanting.

And finally she came again, clamping around my cock, and I followed her, filling her up, both of us slowing as we tried to catch our breath.

"Oh, wow," she whispered.

I slid out of her, rolling so we could hold one another.

"Well, that's a good way to wake up."

She grinned at me, her eyes bright, so full of something that I could barely name. This didn't seem real.

"I have a meeting, and so do you. And then we have dinner with your family. That's not terrifying at all."

I laughed, I couldn't help it. "You've had more dinners with my family recently than I have it seems. You'll be fine."

She looked down at her hand between us, at the diamond ring I had slid over her finger the night before. I had gotten down on one knee, something I didn't think I'd ever do, and asked the love of my life to marry me. It didn't seem real. None of this did.

"You know, the paparazzi's going to find out soon. And the media will go crazy."

"Really?" I asked, not really caring in that moment. I would later. I didn't want people in my private life, and they were already gossiping. People learning that Lark had been dating anyone new had been an explosion of news. One that we were weathering. It would only get worse now, for the moment at least. But in the end, I had Lark, so I would deal with their intrusive need to figure out exactly what I had been through. The Wilders were already under a microscope because of who we had married, who we were marrying. So now I would deal with the next part.

Because Lark was beyond worth it. And I was just glad that I wasn't a dumbass any longer when it came to her.

"They're going to really love taking photos of me glaring at them. One after another, wondering exactly who this guy is that you keep writing songs about."

She laughed, shaking her head against the pillow. "True. They're going to see your scowling face and fall in love, just like I did."

"Well, I am pretty lovable."

I said it so deadpan that she just rolled her eyes and put her hand back on my chest. The light hit the ring again, and I once again took a deep breath, so damn grateful that I had made it out. That we had found one another. Even if it didn't make any sense.

"Anyway, we have to get ready for the day. But I'll see you later?"

"Always. You'll always see me."

We kissed again, and I reminded myself that we really did need to get up, that our lives hadn't stopped just because I had figured out that she was my everything.

We got ready together, both of us talking about a thousand things at once.

"I talked to my parents again, and they'll be out in two weeks."

I ran my hands through my hair, grimacing. "That's not nerve-racking at all."

"You've talked to them over video chat. They love you."

"Sure. They love any guy who gets their daughter stuck in a fire, and then proposes out of the blue."

"It wasn't out of the blue. It might have been fast to some people, but it's been a few months. And now we can finally all meet up and finish the grand unveiling of the spa."

In the few months we had been together, we had worked our asses off on the spa, with a new manager coming in and agreeing with everything that we had already done. We were working it out, and it was no longer my sole responsibility to get it done. For that, I was grateful. The Wilder Retreat and Winery had a thousand other things for me to do.

After I kissed her again, I made it to work, standing side by side with Elliot, as he scowled at his tablet.

"What's wrong?"

"Nothing's wrong. Just work."

"You say that, but you're scowling. You never scowl."

He literally scowled at me just then. "I can do what I want. Just leave me alone."

Elliot stomped off and I just shook my head, confused at what the hell was going on with him.

I would get it out of him, just like he had gotten my anger out of me. My brothers had stood up for me when I couldn't stand up for myself, so we would do this for him.

We were having an early dinner and Wilder meeting, so I cleaned up, excited to see Lark again. There was something seriously wrong with me when I couldn't go a few hours without seeing her.

"Big brother!" a familiar voice said, and I grinned.

My little sister ran towards me, Eliza Wilder-Montgomery, looking radiant as ever.

I opened my arms and she jumped into them, and I spun her around.

People clapped, laughing, as they went about their business. I just shook my head, setting her down on the ground.

"Did I know you were coming in?"

"No, but I had a meeting for my work, and so I was able to come down, but I didn't bring the family." She pouted. "It's so weird traveling without the kids."

"I still think it's so weird that my baby sister's a mom."

She grinned. "I know, right? Of course, I find it weird that you are about to be a husband."

"It's a little scary."

"Yes, but it was scary to you when you found out I was going to be a mom!"

"Damn straight. I'm glad you're here, sis," I said as I wrapped my arm around her shoulder, the two of us making our way towards the main building where we'd have dinner.

"You sound so much lighter. Happier. It's been a long time coming, East. But all of my brothers are healing. It's about damn time."

"We still got one more to go," I said, thinking of Elliot's strange mood.

"And maybe not just him," Eliza whispered.

I frowned as I opened the door to let her go through first. "What do you mean?"

"I don't know, but I'm pretty sure that our branch of the Wilders may be figuring out what we want, but there's another branch that's hurting just as much as we used to."

I thought of our cousins, the ones spread out all over like we had once been, and I sighed. "They've been through hell. But they're okay. They would tell us if they weren't, right?"

Eliza shook her head. "None of us mentioned that we weren't until it was almost too late."

I cursed under my breath. "Well, since we're having a family meeting, we better include all of the family at some point."

Eliza just beamed. "Look at you, sounding all poetic. I blame Lark."

"Blame me for what?" my fiancée asked as she came forward. My heart did that kick thing, and I opened up my other arm so I had my fiancée on one side, and my baby sister on the other. I hugged them close as they laughed with one another, talking a million words a minute.

Each of my brothers stood in the boardroom, a buffet dinner spread out on the sideboard near the main window. Kendall and her team had gone to great lengths to make everything look amazing, and they were damn good at it.

The kids were playing in the corner, Alexis and Eli on the floor with the three of them.

Evan and Kendall stood by the buffet, fixing up the last bits of it. Bethany and Everett stood next to Elijah and Maddie, grinning at one another.

And Elliot stood at the window, glass of wine in hand as he stared off into the distance at the Hill Country. I wanted to see his face, wanted to ask what was wrong. But not yet. Tonight was about planning for the future, celebrating. And then we could start laying the groundwork for Elliot, and maybe our cousins, if they let us.

I hadn't always been the steady Wilder, I had just been a man that was good with his hands. But this family had changed me. For the better, even when I thought it was for the worst.

I still couldn't believe that this was my luck. That this was who I got to be.

"Why do you look so sad?" Lark asked as Eliza went off to speak with Elliot, hopefully bringing him out of his mood.

"Just thinking about how far we've come."

"You guys were six brothers with a dream, and now look at you."

I shook my head, laughing. "Eli had the dream. We just followed because we didn't have anything else to do. I assumed I'd work at a hardware store, or bagging groceries. I had a degree, but I didn't know what to do with it. I got out too early."

"But you got out, and you had people to lean on."

I looked down at her and smiled. "Yeah. And I guess you're one of them."

She just rolled her eyes. "I guess I am. Now, let's go have dinner with the Wilders, show off my beautiful ring, and plan our next adventure."

"Yeah?"

"I don't know what's going to happen next. But I can't wait to stay here for a bit. With you."

I leaned down and brushed my lips against hers as everyone started clapping and catcalling. I flipped them off and ducked Eli's smack to the back of my head, since the kids were in the room. I just laughed and held on to Lark.

We weren't complete yet, weren't finished fixing whatever the hell we needed to. But we were one step closer. And in the end, that's the only thing we needed.

Chapter Twenty-One

Trace

"I'm seriously so glad that you're staying." I turned to Elliot as he spoke, nodded tightly before going back to paying attention to where my feet were. I had been in countless situations where I'd had to have quick footwork. But climbing up and down this hill in the Texas Hill Country meant that I was more likely to trip over a small rock and hurt my ankle. That, or fall into a grouping of cacti. Why there were so many cacti, I wouldn't know. I was used to tall trees that shed their leaves in the winter, and snow on the ground for months on end.

Of course, I had been living in LA and traveling with Bethany around the world for the past few years, so that didn't really happen there either.

"Trace? You okay?"

I turned to Elliot Wilder, pausing to take in the view. "Yeah. Just trying not to fall and get a cactus stuck up my ass."

Elliot paused, stared at me, then burst out laughing.

"Really, cactus up your ass?"

"Shut up," I said with a snort, shaking my head. "That does sound a little pointed though, doesn't it?"

Elliot snorted again, grinning. "Yeah, that doesn't sound like something I want up my ass."

He looked damn good when he laughed, not that I let myself think that often. After all, I had better things to do than watch the way that Elliot smiled. I worked with the Wilders now, and though technically Elliot wasn't my boss, it was still too weird. I didn't need to think about how good the other man looked in jeans, or his usual dress pants.

Plus, I was dating Alicia. We might not be serious, and we might be taking our time, but me taking the time to check out how good Elliot looked when he bent over to tie his shoe? No, didn't need to do that.

"Why the hell are you wearing tennis shoes? You're the one who wanted to go hiking."

We glanced at each other, and this odd, heated moment seemed to fill the air, tension riding us both. It was odd though, because I didn't know if Elliot was into guys. I wasn't even sure that the Wilders knew I was. It wasn't my place to even ask, because I wasn't going to be interested in any of them, I was just going to work with them. And I had been dating Alicia for the past two weeks, and even though we weren't exclusive, I didn't feel like making things complicated.

"Anyway," Elliot said after he cleared his throat and looked off into the distance. "My brother needed my shoes for something, and didn't return them. And since I've wanted to go out on this walk, I'm in tennis shoes. It's fine."

"If you say so," I said, looking at the terrain. "Just be careful."

"Whatever you say, Mom."

"Fuck you."

Elliot turned, looked over his shoulder at me, and winked. "No thanks. You're cute though."

Well, that answered that. We continued our hike, and I did my best not to watch his ass.

We went up the next hill, sweat beading on my forehead. It wasn't too hot, but the sun beat down and it was muggy. I hated muggy.

"So, when do you move in full-time?" Elliot asked.

"In a couple of weeks. Now that the wedding's over and I'm done with setting up the team for the next trip, I'm ready to stay."

"It's going to be weird without you at Bethany's side all the time, isn't it?"

"Trying not to feel guilty, but yeah. Maybe I'm just too old to stand by her side every day. You know?"

"Stop it. You're more in shape than any of the younger guys there. And I say younger guys, because they're like nineteen. You are in your thirties, mister."

"Thanks. You know, I love feeling old."

"Shut up," Elliot said with a laugh. "You're not even a decade older than me."

"Nine years is still a big gap."

And that was good to remember. I was an old man, at least that's how I felt when I was standing next to Elliot. Again, not that it should matter.

"Come on, let's get up on this ridge, take a look at the scenery, then make our way back. Kendall promised dinner tonight."

"I'm getting spoiled with your sister-in-law and all of her food. I need to start hiking more if I'm going to continue to poach off her meals."

Elliot's gaze raked over my body, and I ignored it. Mostly because my cock hurt just thinking about it.

"Whatever you say, old man."

"Fuck you," I said again, and Elliot laughed. He moved to the side, ready to take a step, when the soil shifted.

It happened so quickly, I could barely snap out my arm. I let out a sharp shout, as Elliot's eyes widened and the ground beneath him fell away.

I moved as quickly as I could, reaching for him, but I missed. Instead, Elliot gripped the edge of the embankment, sliding down feet first, as his head slammed into the rock, blood pooling.

"I've got you, I got you. Just hold on, Elliot!" I called out as I crawled towards him, looking over the edge of the cliff.

We weren't on a mountain, but we were still high enough that if Elliot fell, there was no way he was going to make it. Broken legs and arms would be the least of his worries.

Elliot looked up at me, eyes wide. His blood began to drip into his eyes. He blinked it away, fingers digging into the soil, knuckles raw.

"Holy shit. Holy shit."

"Just hold on, I'm going to pull you up."

"The soil's loose. You'll fall right along with me. I'm fine, just go get help."

"Fuck that. I'm coming for you."

Elliot's eyes were a bit wild, but he smirked. "That's what she said."

"Seriously, not the time," I said, even as hysterical

laughter threatened to burble up from my throat. I pushed it away and reached down.

"Just grab my hand."

"If I let go, I'm not going to be able to be strong enough to hold on. I'm fine. I can figure out how to climb up."

"Just grab my hand, Elliot. I've got you. I'm not going to let you fall."

He looked up at me and moved his hand, when the ground beneath me fell away once more.

Bonus Epilogue

Lark

The music blared, people laughed and talked. Drinks were flowing, and others were munching down on the charcuterie boards in front of us.

Awards shows always stressed me out, always worried me, because I felt like I was an impostor. Like I had no right to be here. There were legends here, men and women with dozens of Grammys and other songwriting achievements under their belts. There were dancers and singers and performers. People who were part of my child-hood, and people that were far younger than me now, brightening up the landscape.

There had already been upsets and history being made. Musician after musician, artist after artist had played in front of us, and we had danced and laughed. It had felt like an amazing night.

I had already won three Grammys earlier during the untelevised part of the show. That was fine with me, I actually preferred it. Because while I loved being on stage and performing my songs, being on camera where people watched your face to see how you would react to someone else's win, or dare I say if I won, was not my cup of tea.

We were on the ground floor at tiny tables pressed close together so that way each of the "big" artists sat next to each other, literally rubbing elbows.

I sat at the same table as one of my cowriters from another album, both of us laughing. They had already won four Grammys that night, and were up for Record of the Year and Album of the Year. I was against them in both of those categories, but I knew I wasn't going to win. There was no possible way. I was perfectly fine not winning anything, literally just being nominated was a huge thing.

But the next award I was the most nervous about.

Song of the Year—the songwriter award.

I had never won it before, though I had been nominated. This was where my heart was, and I honestly did not want to win. Because that meant I had to go up on stage, and I did not want to deal.

East was next to me, gripping my hand. He didn't want to be here either, but he was. Because he loved me.

The fact that he was my *husband*, and we were learning this relationship of ours together, meant the world to me. It seemed so surreal that this was my life now. I was a married woman and people constantly wanted to know more about what East and I were doing. They wanted to know about our courtship, about the Wilders, about my friendship with Bethany. They wanted to know about who East had been and who he was now. They wanted to know every inch of my life.

But they didn't know the truth. They didn't know us. And I was truly happy with that. We could ignore the noise and just be together. I had notebooks full of songs that were about us—most would never see the light of day.

I had even more notebooks about others who weren't real. I wrote about love, life, hope, darkness, and grief. I wrote about the emotions and lives that I lived in life and in dreams.

The cameras kept getting too close to East's face, and he would glare, then he would look at me and relax. And that was better than any reward.

"You're going to kick ass!" Adelay said from my side, as she kissed my cheek. "I'm rooting for you."

"I feel like I don't know what I'm doing," I said with a laugh.

She looked over my shoulder at East, who was with a seven-time Grammy Award-winning R&B artist, the two of them talking in low tones, smiling.

"You see, you've already kicked some ass. He's cute. Congratulations by the way, on the wedding. I'm sorry I couldn't make it."

"It's really okay. We liked it small."

"So the fact that I got an invite at all made me feel amazing. But I was on set and couldn't get away. I tried, though."

"I know you did. Just like I tried to make it to your wedding and was stuck in a hurricane."

She rolled her eyes. "Doing things quickly and under the radar isn't easy. But you're going to be amazing. I can't wait to see you stand up there."

"It's not going to be me. Have you heard the other songs? No, I'm just fine here."

"Whatever you say, Lark."

And then East was tugging on me, gesturing. "I think it's up. Right?"

I cupped his cheek, my fingers sliding over his soft beard. "I love you."

"Yeah? I love you too. I'm so fucking proud of you."

I laughed, knowing the cameras had probably picked up his cursing and the way that we had our foreheads pressed to each other. But then he kissed me, softly so it wouldn't mess up my makeup, and I sighed into him.

People clapped around us, and I knew I had to be better than this. I didn't want our lives to be so public, and I probably should have found a better way to do this, but it was fine.

And then the cameras were rolling again, and the presenter had an envelope in their hand.

"And for best Song of the Year, the winner is 'Heading East,' written and sung by Lark Thornbird."

It was as if there was a cacophony of sound in my ears, echoing where I couldn't breathe.

Adelay was squeezing my shoulders, screaming as she stood up and clapped. Everybody was standing and coming towards me, the cameras on my face. But all I could do was stare at East.

"Oh my God."

"Well. I guess if you had to write a song about me, you getting a Grammy for it is okay. Now go stand up there, baby. You earned this. And so much more."

And then he kissed me hard on the mouth as cameras flashed. I held onto him, my knees shaking as I tried to make my way up to the stage.

And when I stood up there, Grammy in hand thanking everybody that I could, I only had eyes for him.

Because he had stayed. He had always been there.

And I would always be there for him.

He was my East star. He was mine.

And for the first time in my life, I was grateful I had written a song about the man in my heart. And the man that was forever mine.

NEXT IN THE WILDER BROTHERS SERIES:
Trace, Elliot, and Sidney get their story in
FINDING THE ROAD TO US.

A Note from Carrie Ann Ryan

Thank you so much for reading **STAY HERE WITH ME.**

After so many romances, this was my first time writing a singer songwriter and now I have the bug! I really want to write more singers and rockstars...and Lark might just be my jumping off point!

This romance was about resting and figuring out who you are. I've watched people come back home from traumatic experiences and not know where home could be. Having friends (and myself) search to find themselves taught me who I needed to be in this world.

East and Lark's romance was hot and intense and yet sweet at the same time. And I'm so glad that they got the help they needed.

This is only the start for the Wilders, and I thank you for going on this journey...and I can't wait to keep going!

The Wilder Brothers Series:

Book 1: One Way Back to Me

Book 2: Always the One for Me

Book 3: The Path to You

Book 4: Coming Home for Us

Book 5: Stay Here With Me

Book 6: Finding the Road to Us

Book 7: Moments for You

Book 8: A Wilder Wedding

NEXT IN THE WILDER BROTHERS SERIES:
Trace, Elliot, and Sidney get their story in
FINDING THE ROAD TO US.

IF YOU'D LIKE TO READ A BONUS SCENE FROM EAST AND LARK:
CHECK OUT THIS SPECIAL EPILOGUE!

If you want to make sure you know what's coming next from me, you can sign up for my newsletter at www. CarrieAnnRyan.com; follow me on twitter at @CarrieAnnRyan, or like my Facebook page. I also have a

Facebook Fan Club where we have trivia, chats, and other goodies. You guys are the reason I get to do what I do and I thank you.

Make sure you're signed up for my MAILING LIST so you can know when the next releases are available as well as find giveaways and FREE READS.

Happy Reading!

Also from Carrie Ann Ryan

The Montgomery Ink Legacy Series:
Book 1: Bittersweet Promises
Book 2: At First Meet
Book 2.5: Happily Ever Never
Book 3: Longtime Crush
Book 4: Best Friend Temptation
Book 5: Last First Kiss
Book 6: His Second Chance

The Wilder Brothers Series:
Book 1: One Way Back to Me
Book 2: Always the One for Me
Book 3: The Path to You
Book 4: Coming Home for Us

Book 5: Stay Here With Me
Book 6: Finding the Road to Us
Book 7: Moments for You
Book 8: A Wilder Wedding

The First Time Series:
Book 1: Good Time Boyfriend
Book 2: Last Minute Fiancé

The Aspen Pack Series:
Book 1: Etched in Honor
Book 2: Hunted in Darkness
Book 3: Mated in Chaos
Book 4: Harbored in Silence
Book 5: Marked in Flames

The Montgomery Ink: Fort Collins Series:
Book 1: Inked Persuasion
Book 2: Inked Obsession
Book 3: Inked Devotion
Book 3.5: Nothing But Ink
Book 4: Inked Craving
Book 5: Inked Temptation

The Montgomery Ink: Boulder Series:
Book 1: Wrapped in Ink

Book 2: Sated in Ink
Book 3: Embraced in Ink
Book 3: Moments in Ink
Book 4: Seduced in Ink
Book 4.5: Captured in Ink
Book 4.7: Inked Fantasy
Book 4.8: A Very Montgomery Christmas

Montgomery Ink: Colorado Springs

Book 1: Fallen Ink
Book 2: Restless Ink
Book 2.5: Ashes to Ink
Book 3: Jagged Ink
Book 3.5: Ink by Numbers

Montgomery Ink Denver:

Book 0.5: Ink Inspired
Book 0.6: Ink Reunited
Book 1: Delicate Ink
Book 1.5: Forever Ink
Book 2: Tempting Boundaries
Book 3: Harder than Words
Book 3.5: Finally Found You
Book 4: Written in Ink
Book 4.5: Hidden Ink
Book 5: Ink Enduring

Also from Carrie Ann Ryan

Book 6: <u>Ink Exposed</u>
Book 6.5: <u>Adoring Ink</u>
Book 6.6: <u>Love, Honor, & Ink</u>
Book 7: <u>Inked Expressions</u>
Book 7.3: <u>Dropout</u>
Book 7.5: <u>Executive Ink</u>
Book 8: <u>Inked Memories</u>
Book 8.5: <u>Inked Nights</u>
Book 8.7: <u>Second Chance Ink</u>
Book 8.5: Montgomery Midnight Kisses
Bonus: Inked Kingdom

The On My Own Series:

Book 0.5: My First Glance
Book 1: My One Night
Book 2: My Rebound
Book 3: My Next Play
Book 4: My Bad Decisions

The Promise Me Series:

Book 1: Forever Only Once
Book 2: From That Moment
Book 3: Far From Destined
Book 4: From Our First

The Less Than Series:

Book 1: Breathless With Her
Book 2: Reckless With You
Book 3: Shameless With Him

The Fractured Connections Series:

Book 1: Breaking Without You
Book 2: Shouldn't Have You
Book 3: Falling With You
Book 4: Taken With You

The Whiskey and Lies Series:

Book 1: <u>Whiskey Secrets</u>
Book 2: <u>Whiskey Reveals</u>
Book 3: <u>Whiskey Undone</u>

The Gallagher Brothers Series:

Book 1: <u>Love Restored</u>
Book 2: <u>Passion Restored</u>
Book 3: <u>Hope Restored</u>

The Ravenwood Coven Series:

Book 1: Dawn Unearthed
Book 2: Dusk Unveiled
Book 3: Evernight Unleashed

The Talon Pack:

Also from Carrie Ann Ryan

Book 1: Tattered Loyalties

Book 2: An Alpha's Choice

Book 3: Mated in Mist

Book 4: Wolf Betrayed

Book 5: Fractured Silence

Book 6: Destiny Disgraced

Book 7: Eternal Mourning

Book 8: Strength Enduring

Book 9: Forever Broken

Book 10: Mated in Darkness

Book 11: Fated in Winter

Redwood Pack Series:

Book 1: An Alpha's Path

Book 2: A Taste for a Mate

Book 3: Trinity Bound

Book 3.5: A Night Away

Book 4: Enforcer's Redemption

Book 4.5: Blurred Expectations

Book 4.7: Forgiveness

Book 5: Shattered Emotions

Book 6: Hidden Destiny

Book 6.5: A Beta's Haven

Book 7: Fighting Fate

Book 7.5: Loving the Omega

Book 7.7: The Hunted Heart

Book 8: <u>Wicked Wolf</u>

The Elements of Five Series:

Book 1: From Breath and Ruin

Book 2: From Flame and Ash

Book 3: From Spirit and Binding

Book 4: From Shadow and Silence

Dante's Circle Series:

Book 1: <u>Dust of My Wings</u>

Book 2: <u>Her Warriors' Three Wishes</u>

Book 3: <u>An Unlucky Moon</u>

Book 3.5: <u>His Choice</u>

Book 4: <u>Tangled Innocence</u>

Book 5: <u>Fierce Enchantment</u>

Book 6: <u>An Immortal's Song</u>

Book 7: <u>Prowled Darkness</u>

Book 8: Dante's Circle Reborn

Holiday, Montana Series:

Book 1: <u>Charmed Spirits</u>

Book 2: <u>Santa's Executive</u>

Book 3: <u>Finding Abigail</u>

Book 4: <u>Her Lucky Love</u>

Book 5: Dreams of Ivory

Also from Carrie Ann Ryan

The Branded Pack Series:
(Written with Alexandra Ivy)

Book 1: <u>Stolen and Forgiven</u>

Book 2: <u>Abandoned and Unseen</u>

Book 3: <u>Buried and Shadowed</u>

About the Author

Carrie Ann Ryan is the New York Times and USA Today bestselling author of contemporary, paranormal, and young adult romance. Her works include the Montgomery Ink, Redwood Pack, Fractured Connections, and Elements of Five series, which have sold over 3.0 million books worldwide. She started writing while in graduate school for her advanced degree in chemistry and hasn't stopped since. Carrie Ann has written over seventy-five novels and novellas with more in the works. When she's not losing herself in her emotional and action-packed worlds, she's reading as much as she can while wrangling her clowder of cats who have more followers than she does.

www.CarrieAnnRyan.com